Bodies in Trouble

Previously Published

"Bodies in Trouble," *Building Community* anthology
"The Garden," *Riddle Fence*, Issue #37
"Dead Reckoning," *The Fiddlehead*, Issue #282
"Me and Mom and Uncle John," *Riddle Fence*, Issue #30
"Patsy's Kitchen," *Other Voices*, Volume #12, Number 1

Bodies in Trouble

Diane Carley

Editor: Susan Musgrave
Cover art: Kristin MacPherson
Book and cover design: Tania Wolk, Third Wolf Studio
Printed and bound in Canada at Friesens, Altona, MB

The publisher gratefully acknowledges the support of Creative Saskatchewan, the Canada Council for the Arts and SK Arts.

Library and Archives Canada Cataloguing in Publication

Title: Bodies in trouble / Diane Carley.
Names: Carley, Diane, author.
Description: Short stories.
Identifiers: Canadiana (print) 20220213194 |
Canadiana (ebook) 20220214212 | ISBN 9781989274736
(softcover) | ISBN 9781989274743 (PDF)
Classification: LCC PS8605.A7445 B63 2022 | DDC C813/.6—dc23

radiant press

Box 33128 Cathedral PO
Regina, SK S4T 7X2
info@radiantpress.ca
www.radiantpress.ca

For Sarah, always.

Me and Mom and Uncle John

ME AND MOM AND UNCLE JOHN are watching porn in his living room. Mom is divorced. John has a beard. I am twelve years old.

Aunt May went to bed early, as if she was tired, as if there was nothing wrong. My uncle sits in an olive-green armchair to the right of the screen, my mother on the couch behind him. I sit at the dining room table.

I see everything.

I see the pasty blonde in a dreary kitchen open the door to a uniformed man with a box in his arms. I see her, a couple of suggestive comments later, bent over the table with the deliveryman behind her. I see my mother sitting stolidly on the couch staring forward as Uncle John lounges in his chair watching the couple's relentless rhythm.

I hear the steady humming clatter of the film reel turning, the pitiful barely-there dialogue and the endless wet sounds of the man and woman doing what neither appears to be enjoying, despite much licking of lips and lolling of heads. They grimace the way my friend Tammy did when her mother pulled a sliver from her finger.

Uncle John and Aunt May have no children. May is my mother's older sister. If I had a sister, I'd never fight with her. But Mom and Aunt May argue all the time.

"Oh, for Christ's sake, May, who died and made you God?"

"That's hardly the kind of language to be using around the child, June."

Aunt May always refers to me as the child, as if that captures all that I am and all I ever will be. Even when she speaks to me directly, it's "Eat your beans, child. Come on child, get a move on."

I don't know why she and Uncle John don't have kids of their own. All I know is that it makes for a boring visit. We don't see them often but this year we've made the five-hour trip twice. When Mom says we're going again, I say, "No, I don't want to. There's nothing to do there. Why do we have to go?"

"We don't have to go, Janis. It's family, we want to go."

"Well, I don't want to go. And I don't know why you do. You always call Aunt May a pompous blowhard."

"When...never mind. It doesn't matter. Sometimes we get angry with people. I get mad at you too, Janis, but it doesn't mean I leave you behind and never see you again, now does it?"

On the drive to Aunt May and Uncle John's house, Mom won't let me play Sly and the Family Stone on the 8-track. Instead, we listen to some old lady singer moaning about her stupid sad life. I'm almost happy to see Aunt May's house after hours of listening to quivering voices, acoustic guitars and the start and stop stutter of my mother's singing. Humming, then breaking into song at the chorus or some other random phrase, always a beat behind but making up for it with sheer volume.

Mom honks the horn as we pull into the driveway of the ranch-style bungalow. Aunt May comes out and stands on the concrete porch, crossing her arms across her chest, her dark eyes staring at us as we climb out of the station wagon my mom bought the year before from our next- door neighbour.

Aunt May is head cashier at the Loblaws down the street. Uncle John is a college professor who was laid off the summer before.

Something to do with math.

Something to do with a girl.

"Hi, hi," says Mom.

"Hello, June. Well, well, look at you, child. Don't you keep growing like a weed? Go on in now. John's in the basement but he'll be right up. Now, June, you didn't go and bring..."

I let the screen door slam behind me shutting out the rest of Aunt May's words and carry my bag to the room I share with my mom at the end of a long hallway off the living room. The house is quiet, muffled, as if the walls are covered in cotton batting. Dropping my stuff by the bed I turn around to find Uncle John standing in the doorway. He wears dark blue track pants and a faded t-shirt with I Heart NY emblazoned across his chest.

"Howdy, Junior, how goes the battle?" he says, stroking his beard.

When he turns towards the sound of Mom and Aunt May banging their way into the house, I duck past him and scoot over to my mother. She is arguing with Aunt May about the box of food we brought with us. Wilting lettuce, bruised bananas, and bordering-on-mouldy grapes from our fridge.

"It was just going to go bad at home."

"So you decided to bring it all this way to rot here?"

"Well no, May, I thought we might eat it."

"If you didn't eat it at home, what makes you think you're going to eat it now that it's sat in a hot car all day?"

"Honestly, I can never do anything right around you...Oh hi, John," my mother says in that high girly tone I hate.

I slip out the door and sit down on the porch steps, staring at the driveway next door where a teenage boy is now hunched under the hood of a car, his hands plucking at the engine.

My mother and Aunt May continue to bicker in the kitchen. I glance back towards their voices only to see Uncle John lurking in the front hall. I wander over to the neighbours' and Uncle John retreats into the house.

Where we live, the only hints that we'd just come through the sixties are the reverberating, echoey sound of "I'd Love to Change the World" playing on my friend Tracy's transistor radio, and our English teacher Mr. Spellman's bellbottom slacks. Meadowville, a town with fewer than a thousand people, is closer to Algonquin Park than it is to Toronto, so it has no music festivals, demonstrations, or love-ins.

Nor does it have any black people. Which is why I am curious about Aunt May and Uncle John's new neighbours. The mother is an emergency room nurse and the father is a high school chemistry teacher. They have three sons. Jimmy is the youngest. He's the one working on the car.

I stand on the edge of their driveway and say hi.

He smiles at me, then turns his attention back to the engine.

"Is there something wrong with it?"

"Nah, just changing the spark plugs."

I nod like I know what they are.

"Are they broken?"

"No, you just gotta change them regularly to keep the engine working proper. Most people don't."

He struggles with something under the hood then his hand jerks up. Stepping towards me, he holds out a small object in the palm of his hand. It's got thick white plastic with writing in the middle and the ends are narrow with tight metallic ridges.

"If there's a problem with a spark plug, the car will start running rough. Not a big deal. But you wouldn't want one blowing out when you were driving down a highway."

"What would happen?" I ask, reaching out to touch it.

"Janis, get in here."

My mother stands on the stoop, her arm stretched out stiffly holding the door open.

Jimmy closes his hand over the spark plug, walks back to the car and slams the hood down.

The screen door bangs twice against the frame as he disappears inside his house.

"What?"

"Leave the neighbours alone."

"Why? I wasn't doing anything wrong."

"Just get inside, Janis."

I march into the living room and plop down on the couch. Uncle John sits in his armchair under the window, reading. He smirks at me as he flips through the pages of his magazine.

Aunt May calls me into the kitchen to set the table for dinner. Piling the placemats in my arms, she points to the cutlery drawer. I meander into the dining room and lay the white woven placemats on the scarred but polished oak table. Outside, kids are playing street hockey and a young boy drags an orange kite that never rises above his head no matter how fast he runs.

Aunt May catches me gazing out the window. She holds up the knife and fork at one of the settings and crosses her arms to place them back down on opposite sides.

"Knife on the right. Fork on the left."

I switch the remaining cutlery, then turn towards the living room.

"Uh uh. I need you to get plates and glasses too. And fill them with water before you put them on the table. Thank you," she says in a perky clipped voice.

"No, June, not that wine. Take the red that's on the counter."

"I'd rather have white."

"We're having beef, June. Put the red on the table, please. The wine glasses are on the shelf above the sink. John, dinnertime. Child, grab the napkins from the hutch. Alright, here we go," she says setting a platter of sliced beef in the middle of the table.

"June, grab the mashed potatoes. And the peas," says Aunt May.

She gestures for me to sit at the spot to her right then runs back into the kitchen. "No, no, the serving spoons are in this drawer. Here, take these."

My mother comes back into the dining room, a tight smile on her face as she places the vegetables on the table. John helps himself to meat.

"Beef's a little well done," he says, continuing to eat while the rest of us spoon food onto our plates. "No gravy?"

"Oh my gosh, June, did you not fill the gravy boat from the pan on the stove?" Aunt May asks.

"No. You didn't..."

"Never mind, I'll get it," Aunt May says, scurrying into the kitchen.

Mom rolls her eyes at me as Aunt May returns with a brimming container, which she hands to Uncle John. He pours a small river over his meat and potatoes.

My mother holds her hand out for the gravy boat, but Uncle John doesn't notice and sets it down on the edge of his placemat.

"Wine?" Aunt May asks.

Uncle John holds up his glass and she walks to the end of the table to fill it for him.

"June?"

"No, thank you," says my mother pursing her lips.

Aunt May fills up her own wine glass then hands the bowl of Brussels sprouts to me.

"No, thank you."

"Try just a little," she says, putting a small spoonful onto my plate. I look to my mother, but she pointedly ignores us all.

I push the Brussels sprouts to the edge so they're not touching any other food.

"My god, but that's some fierce wind they got down south," Aunt May continues. "A tornado touched down in Alabama, they say. Tossed a trailer around like it was a big old piece of fluff. Seven people killed and still counting."

Aunt May shakes her head like those people chose a bad way to live and it's sad it all came down so hard for them.

"Pass the peas."

"Such a shame," she says, handing the bowl to Uncle John.

I finish everything except the dreaded sprouts.

"So, John, you ever been caught in a storm like that?" my mother asks.

"Nope," Uncle John says, scooping more food onto his plate. He turns to me. "You got a boyfriend?"

"NO."

"What about that boy next door? You and him seemed cozy."

"Leave the child alone, John," says Aunt May.

"What? I'm just asking."

My mother glares at him while Aunt May tops up her wine glass. He smiles at me and laughs. Uncle John often laughs when things aren't funny.

Aunt May tells me I have to stay at the table until I finish my Brussels sprouts. We don't have those kinds of rules at our house.

"Mom?"

My mother ignores me as she carries the leftover food into the kitchen. Uncle John goes into the living room and turns on the television. Aunt May briskly stacks the dishes, the clank of disapproval from cutlery dropped onto empty plates mingling with the tinny canned laughter from the TV, as I slouch in front of the six half-moons of baby cabbage scattered about my gravy flecked plate.

After the kitchen is cleaned, everyone but me goes into the living room. I'm still at the table in front of my plate of cold food when Uncle John pulls out a screen and projector. That's when Aunt May says she's going to bed even though it's just after eight. I don't know what's coming. Then I do.

My mother tells me to go to my room but I stay put, curious to see what comes next. I feel strange stirrings laced with disgust at the sight of adults having sex. Confused and disturbed by the sensations, I slip outside and sit on the stoop. My mother tells me not to wander off.

Outside, it's cool and dark. I kick at the metal rail on the steps to the driveway and watch the Robinsons' house where a light shines in the carport. I walk over and knock on the door.

Jimmy answers. He stands in the centre of the doorway, the light from inside framing his tall lean body.

"Hi," I say.

I hadn't thought beyond knocking. I assume I will be invited in. That's what happens when I go to my friends' houses. But Jimmy remains where he is.

Standing at the threshold of his house, wondering what it's like inside, it reminds me of the first time I went on a plane. It was the year before Mom and Dad split and we'd flown to Florida for Christmas. We rented a car at the airport and on our way to the condo we stopped at a grocery store. The quiet whoosh of automatic doors opened to reveal a cavern of frigid brightness, then they closed behind us, trapping the cold inside. While my mother and father strolled the massive aisles of the dazzlingly well-lit store, I stood mesmerized by the candy in the racks by the cash registers. They were unlike any I'd seen before with their strange names like Milky Way, Butterfingers, and Babe Ruth.

Everything about that trip felt familiar yet odd. There were decorations and tinsel and carols playing in the malls, but no snow, no toques, no tree in our apartment. It was sunny and sandy and bright. But it wasn't Christmas. That was our last holiday together. I don't see much of Dad now that he's moved to Alberta.

"Is your mom here?" I ask, unable to come up with a better reason for knocking on Jimmy's door.

"Nope. Just me."

"Oh."

"I can tell her you were looking for her."

"No, I..."

I feel stupid standing there. I can't go forward and I can't go back. The flashing light of a television pulses from the kitchen window to the left of the doorway where Jimmy stands, unmoving.

"You should go home," he says.

When I walk back into the living room John is now sitting on the couch beside my mother. She glances up at me and shifts in her seat. Then she turns her attention back to the screen and I go down the hallway to our room, trailed by the fading moans and groans of the movie. I don't hear my mother come to bed.

The next morning is overcast, a dull light slipping in through the sheer curtains over my bed. I listen to the sounds of people starting their day. Water courses through the pipes in the wall as the whirr of a blender and raised voices leak in from the hallway. When the sounds stop, I turn over and open my eyes. Uncle John stands beside my bed.

"Morning."

I sit up and pull the covers to my chest. He stoops towards me.

"So, looks like you're sticking around a couple of extra days. Won't that be fun?"

"What's going on?" my mother asks poking her head in the door.

"I was telling Janis about the change of plans."

"Mom?"

"I'll leave you to it," he says, leaving the room.

"It's just a couple of days, Janis."

"I don't want to."

"Too bad. Get dressed."

After she leaves, I burrow under the covers. Then, I think I hear a creaking noise. Afraid it's Uncle John, I leap up. But there's no one there. Grabbing some clothes, I go into the washroom to change. When I come out, my mom's standing at the hallway closet, pulling out a towel.

"I don't like it here," I say. "Aunt May's so bossy and Uncle John keeps creeping up on me all the time."

"Don't be ridiculous."

"I want to go home."

"That's enough, Janis. Go eat your breakfast."

Aunt May sits alone at the kitchen table. She looks up at me then turns away. I feel my face flush. I can tell that she heard me.

I stand by the sink, unsure what to do.

"June," Aunt May says, when my mother walks into the room, "You need to go home."

"Why should I?" my mother asks like a child being told to clean up another child's mess. "John invited us to stay another couple of days."

"I'm sure he did. But I don't think that's a very good idea," she says. "Do you?"

My mom shifts her weight from one foot to the other as Aunt May stares at her. When Mom doesn't say anything, Aunt May turns and heads downstairs to the basement.

"Honestly, she's impossible," my mother says, pacing around the kitchen. "Who does she think she is, anyway? I need a cigarette."

"I'm going over to Jimmy's," I blurt out.

"What?" My mother furrows her brow.

"He invited me into his house last night."

"Is that right?"

"I didn't go in. But maybe I will this time," I say, trying to punish her, to annoy her, to get her to leave, to do something, anything.

"You are not to go over there. Do you hear me?" she calls as I let the screen door slam behind me.

Running towards the park across the street, I feel bad, unable to look at the house next door. After wandering past boys on skateboards, girls playing soccer, and kids splashing in the wading pool, I sit on a wooden swing and run my toes along the grooves already made in the sandy ground.

I lean back and move my legs back and forth, pushing the swing higher and higher. I feel the breeze against my face as I look up at the sky, open and blue, no clouds. Then, as I'm kicking upwards, the seat does a little drop in the air, a heart-thumping pause that tells me I've gone too far. I stop pumping my legs, letting them dangle free, as the swing falls back into its groove, and starts slowing down.

I jump off, take a quick look around to make sure no one is watching, and fling the seat so hard it flips over the top bar, its chains clanging against the steel. I do this again and again, winding the swing all the way around, until I can't reach it anymore. I do the same thing to the next one and the one beside it, then step back and watch them all swinging impotently in the air.

"Hey," a man yells, pointing his arm at me.

Taking off in the opposite direction, I don't stop running until I've put three blocks between him and me. I crouch down, panting heavily, and glance over my shoulder. Nobody is after me. Feeling a shot of energy from getting away with it, I stride down the street as if I am innocent, as if I have done nothing wrong.

The air in Aunt May and Uncle John's house is heavy, like in those sweltering moments before lightning cracks open the night sky.

My mother and Uncle John stand together in the living room with her bag at her feet. She reaches out to touch his forearm. He pulls away from her and looks at me.

"There you are," my mother says, withdrawing her hand.

"Are we leaving?"

"Yes, I've decided we should go home after all. See if we can still get you into that summer camp you wanted."

"The deadline was last week."

"We can try."

"I already told you it's too late."

"Don't be so negative," she says looking up at Uncle John with her see-what-I-have-to-put-up-with look.

He winks at me.

"Go pack your bag, Janis," my mother says. "I'll meet you at the car."

"But I haven't eaten."

"You should have thought of that before."

I pack quickly, before she changes her mind, grateful that we're leaving, no matter what the reason. At the front door, Uncle John reaches for my bag, but I pull it close, turning my back on him. He follows me outside.

"Well, I guess this is it," Mom says.

We stand there awkwardly for a few moments. She steps towards Uncle John. But he turns and walks towards the house.

She hesitates, then reaches into her purse for her keys. Jimmy appears in his doorway. I lift my hand to wave to him, but he slips back into the interior as Uncle John mounts the porch steps.

My mother and I climb into the station wagon to begin the long drive home.

Bodies in Trouble

AT NIGHT, ALONE, when I'm thinking of something else, it appears. The shock of light across the windshield, the dark silhouette behind twin beams, the speeding blur in front of me. Then silence.

Each time, I wait to see taillights or hear a crash, a squeal, anything to shatter my belief that it was nothing but a beatific illusion. And every time, I'm rewarded with the comforting sight of an unbroken white line down the middle of the road leading to a point forever out of reach, everything whole and pure and intact, the way it should be.

THE FIRST TIME it happened was ten years ago, the night of my best friend Becky's eighteenth birthday. We'd been planning her party for weeks. She was beyond excited, grinning wildly every time the doorbell rang. When a gaggle of boys walked in, she whispered "Which one do you want?"

But I didn't want a boy. I wanted her. I'd wanted her since she said, "You know what I've always wanted to do" and then she kissed me.

We'd been drinking a bottle of cheap bubbly wine that I stole from my sister's bedroom. We giggled and wrestled and kissed some more, then fell asleep in our clothes.

The next morning, she pretended nothing happened. She kept saying how drunk she'd been, how the whole night was a blur. I remembered everything. My world turned upside down but hers stayed the same.

The night of her birthday, I smuggled a bottle of Baby Duck in my overnight bag, hoping to recreate the moment I'd relived in my mind a hundred times. I figured we'd drink it after her parents went to bed.

Once everyone left, we headed upstairs. I went into the bathroom and when I came out, she was gone. She was not in her bedroom or in the hall. I tiptoed towards the stairs. She sat on the bottom step quietly speaking into the phone.

I knew she was talking to that guy Rick who'd been hanging around her all night. She asked him to come back. She said her parents were asleep and she'd let him in the side door. When she went into the kitchen, I slipped outside and drove away.

It was a clear evening, a smattering of stars shining against the dark sky. The moon was high, a sliver of crescent light. I felt a small burst of exhilaration steal through my misery.

Nobody knew I was not where I was supposed to be.

The road glistened in the cold night air, fallow farmland stretching for miles on either side. I'd seen few cars, the distant arc of bright lights clicked down to a dull shine as I drew near, the high-speed whine, like a turbo-charged mosquito, storming past my ear. Then nothing until the next faint glow from far away.

There hadn't been a car for several minutes when suddenly there were lights passing across the road in front of me. Then they were gone, and it was as if they never existed. I kept driving.

That could not have been a car crossing in front of me. There's no way it crashed into the ditch, I thought. Just as years later, I told myself that everything was fine between Lynne and me.

WE MET THE NIGHT she stepped into my cab with a black eye, a battered suitcase, and no idea where she was going.

"I have forty bucks," she said. "Just drive until it's gone."

"Which way?"

She stared out the side window and waved vaguely to the east.

I stole glances at her in my rear-view mirror, but she kept her head down, the hints of red in her straight, shoulder-length blonde hair glinting in the light from passing cars.

It was a quiet night, not much coming over the radio except the occasional rush of static and garbled dispatch chatter. I turned onto the highway. She didn't look up, even when I started zooming in and out of four lanes of never-say-die traffic. When I hit the edge of the mega metropolis, in that lonely place between the core and the suburbs, the cars became fewer and further between. I pulled into an all-night cafe.

"Is this it? Is the trip over?" she asked.

"No, I'm just stopping for a coffee. Come on, I'll buy you one."

She hesitated. Then followed me inside. The place smelled of burnt toast, damp rags, and cinnamon. The only other customers were a pair of old men at the counter, and a guy with long greasy hair staring at his reflection in the window.

We sat in a booth near the back. I bought her a jumbo black coffee and an apple fritter. By the time she was on her third cup and her second donut, she seemed to be waking from a deep sleep.

"Are you alright?" I asked.

She reached towards her bruised eye, then let her hand drop to the table.

"You know, I always wanted to be a pilot," she said. "Imagine being able to fly anywhere in the world. First place I'd go is Greece. I'd love to see all those whitewashed houses and water so blue it doesn't look real. Only trouble is, I might never come back."

She turned towards me, her eyes a faded green.

"What about you?" she asked.

"What about me?"

"What do you dream about?"

I shrugged. My dreams were not really the good kind.

"It would be fun to drive on the autobahn," I said. "There's no speed limit, so it would be like flying without a plane."

"Aren't we an odd pair of ducks wanting to break free of our earthly chains," she said, dropping back into herself.

I took her home with me. She had nowhere else to go. She seemed vaguely grateful but not surprised. I set her up on the living room couch. In the middle of the night, she crawled in beside me. She lay in my arms weary and worn, while I puffed up proud like a battle-scarred knight who has rescued the princess. From then on, she slept with me, in time becoming my lover.

That summer, we rented a cabin on the edge of a lake near Bracebridge. We swam and frolicked and did what all girls in love do, believing it would never end.

On our last night, we huddled together at the campfire, the silence thick as syrup, the sky deep and dark, far from the diffuse glow of city lights. I sat propped against a log with Lynne snuggling into my chest. The smell of her strawberry shampoo mingled with the cool scent of night air and the smoky tang of the fire.

"Wouldn't it be great to float up in the sky and watch the world from a star?" she asked.

"Not really, since you'd be dead."

"Where's your sense of wonder?"

"Even if you did survive, you'd never be able to see anything down here. Do you have any idea how far away those stars are?"

"Come on, let yourself go. Imagine us floating up there, together."

I shut my eyes, trying to envision us drifting through space as she clasped my arms tighter around her.

I squirmed out of her grasp, adjusted my position, then pulled her close again. The trick was to get comfortable again after every shift.

As the fire faded into flickering spurts of orange and red, neither one of us moved to put on another log. The circle of warmth in which we were sheltered, dissolved, leaving us chilled.

I threw water on the dying flames, the angry hiss of steam shooting up from the splashed coals. We entered the cabin, the hollow bang of the screen door echoing behind us. The cold air on our naked skins sent us tumbling under the covers. I turned on my side and she curled up behind me, her hand tucked between my breasts. The bedsprings creaked as we settled and I slipped into that melting place between waking and sleeping, where sensations are slow and peaceful, like swimming in a calm, quiet lake.

Soon after returning to real life, though, my stroke faltered. There wasn't one simple cause. It was the dull drip of time, the steady cascade of annoyances pocking my spirit. It was the asshole in a suit who stiffed me. The ever-shifting current of Lynne's moods. Her reduced hours at the flower shop. She said it would give her more time for her poetry. I asked if it would also give her more time to figure out how to pay the rent.

I recognized this landscape. I'd been here before. The dismay of leaking love. Attention splintering in new directions. The deadening familiarity.

A few years back, I had a girlfriend whose high fluttery giggle I once found sweet and childlike. Then she started to sound like a demented Betty Boop. One day, I went out for pizza, called her from Kingston, and said I didn't think we should see each other anymore.

I've never been a particularly defensive driver, but I am good at leaving the scene.

LIKE THAT NIGHT after Becky's party, when I was tempted to keep driving without looking back, to go all the way to the ocean I'd never even seen.

Instead, I pulled into our driveway, the porch light a faint beacon in the darkness as dread flooded my system. What if it was Rick in that car and I was willing to do nothing, to say nothing, because she wanted him and not me? I spent the weekend in bed, playing the scene over and over in my mind. Trying to convince myself that nothing happened, that I did nothing wrong.

When Rick showed up at school on Monday, I thought it was over. But like the ghost of a guilty conscience, the vision of the vehicle continued to swoop into my mind when I least expected it. The vision I chose not to see, the potential consequences of which, I refused to acknowledge.

JUST AS I CONTINUED to act like nothing was wrong between Lynne and me, that it wasn't my fault her hair smelt like burnt earth as she sat in the dark, drinking tumblers of gin.

As if to convince myself that bliss was still within reach, I tried replicating our time in Bracebridge, conveniently forgetting my doomed attempt at recreating that perfect Baby Duck moment with Becky.

I secretly borrowed a friend's cabin a couple of hours east of the city. While Lynne was out for a walk, I packed our bags and stowed them in my trunk. I suggested we go for a drive. She wanted to stay home and putter in the garden.

"Come on. It's a beautiful day. Just for a bit, then you can have the rest of the day to yourself."

"Fine," she said grudgingly. "As long as I'm back in time for my yoga class."

She pressed her elbow against the car door, put her head in the palm of her hand and stared off into the distance.

"So, is there anything special you want to do this weekend?" I asked.

"You mean besides what I'd planned before you dragged me away?"

"Why are you making such a big deal of it?"

"I'm here. What else do you want?"

"I want you to want to be here. Is that so wrong?"

She smiled at me with weary eyes. I turned my attention to the road ahead.

When we arrived and she realized what I'd done, she tried to create some enthusiasm. I wasn't having any of it, and she soon tired of trying to cheer me up. Of course, I hadn't brought the right clothes for her, the right food. I forgot towels, butter, and books. She browsed through old Equinoxes and stared out at the water. I knew she didn't want to be there, and by that time, I didn't either. But neither of us suggested going home, unable to find our way out of a simple mistake.

That night, I built a campfire. It was a clear evening, the delicate rumbling of frogs and the call of crickets, the only sounds outside the crack and sizzle of burning wood. We sat across from each other, the fire between us, her face appearing wavy and dim through the vapours of heat.

The drive home the next day was long and silent.

I hadn't planned on staying. It's not what I do. But somehow, I slipped past the point of it being easy to leave.

Lynne's pervasive sadness waxed and waned but never completely died out. Sometimes, it was so potent I could tell she was home the second I came through the door, the air thick with misery.

Of course, it might have had something to do with Shelley.

I MET HER AT A PARTY. Lynne wasn't there. She was sick. Again. Shelley and I chatted about movies and cars. She said she'd like a ride in my cab sometime. I said sure and moved on to talk to somebody else. She tracked me down the following week, said she owed me a drink and I owed her a ride. I shrugged and went along.

I often took the path of least resistance. If someone wanted me more than I didn't want them, so it went. The lies came easily. I had to work an extra shift. I was visiting my mother, or I went driving in the rain. Being with Shelley was like being back at the campfire the first time, before the disappointment, the recriminations. It was like driving a dark lonely stretch of highway, safely ensconced in metal and glass and youth.

One afternoon, Lynne and I went to a house-warming party at our friend Rennie's place. It was a rainy miserable fall day, but the new house was cozy and warm. Rennie showed me a coffee table they were finishing. Something they'd found tucked away in the back of a junk shop underneath a mountain of old magazines and butter dishes. They were really proud of their find and wanted to show me every repaired scratch and dent.

"Before you apply a new stain, you gotta sand it down. Take out the rough spots. It's better to do it by hand with a fine grit sandpaper. Gives you more control. But you don't want to over-sand and create gouges or flat spots. Cause then the stain won't soak in right."

In the middle of Rennie's detailed description of sanding techniques, I glanced up and saw Lynne talking to Shelley. Lynne lifted her hand in a desultory wave towards me. I turned my attention back to Rennie. A few minutes later, Lynne came over and said she wanted to leave.

She felt a migraine coming on. I dropped her off at home and said I was going for a drive. She didn't say anything. I left the car running as she climbed out and headed into the house.

I considered returning to the party but instead, I drove out to the

Bluffs. The rain stopped, and it was cold and dreary, so nobody else was around. The last time I was there, Lynne and I had a fight in the parking lot. We never even got out of the car. We yelled at each other, then carried the bitter smell of anger home on our clothes.

I walked to the end of the beach and grabbed a handful of stones. Taking aim at a scrubby tree clinging to the top of the cliff, my throw fell short. I kept trying until one of the stones smacked into the cliff, causing a mini landslide of silt and gravel. I turned from the falling debris to face a punishing wind coming off the lake. A deep chill burrowed beneath my skin.

When I got home, I found Lynne passed out on the couch. Her hand flopped on the floor as if she was in a canoe, lazily trailing her fingers through the water. An overturned glass lay on the carpet pointing to a small wet stain. The air stunk of pot and patchouli. I sat in the chair across from her and gazed at the gentle rise and fall of her breathing, the moon bathing the room in a soft, quiet glow.

When I closed my eyes, the vision came. Beams of light crossing in front of me.

This time, I knew I could not keep driving.

The Garden

MICHAEL CROUCHED on the edge of the garden, a rifle across his lap.

The moon was high. A crescent sliver that appeared and disappeared as clouds swept and swirled across the sky.

He never thought it would come to this. But he didn't know what else to do.

He'd tried everything. Spritzing organic pest repellant on broccoli stalks and tossing fishing nets over cherry trees. He'd built fences and beer moats and scattered eggshell shrapnel to shred bulbous bodies.

For too many nights, Tanya slept alone while he stalked the asparagus bed, scrambling from one failed remedy to another like a man on the run from a swarm of enraged wasps.

And still, his garden was under attack.

That morning, he sliced a dozen banana slugs with a rusty trowel and flung their slimy body parts into the forest. Now, he was after the deer decimating his lettuce.

Michael blamed the lesbians.

IT ALL STARTED when he came home from work one day to announce that he was going to open his own restaurant.

"What happened?" Tanya asked.

"It's perfect. I can create my own food and won't have to suck up to culinary hacks anymore."

"Michael. What did you do?"

"Nothing," he said, rummaging through the liquor cabinet.

Tanya folded her arms across her chest as he poured a shot of whiskey.

"Okay, I may have referred to Randy's rabbit terrine as shit on a stick..."

"You promised you'd stop insulting the chef."

"You didn't see it, Tanya. It was disgusting. I couldn't serve it. Hell, I wouldn't foist it on a pack of wild dogs. Now we can pursue our dream of having our own place."

"Our dream? My dream is to make it through winter without the kids starving to death."

"Way to reach for the stars."

Tanya stood as still as a heron waiting for a fish to come within striking distance, while Michael kicked his foot against the ottoman and rattled coins in his pocket, clouding the waters with his incessant motion.

They'd always had disparate ways of being in the world. Even their exercise regimes were different. She did Pilates and yoga. He drank Scotch and yelled.

Which was how he'd burned all his bridges in the local restaurant scene. Tanya hadn't worked in a kitchen since giving birth to Lisa and Bobby, so they decided that moving to a leaning- towards-trendy town up the coast, to pursue Michael's fantasy, was a more solid prospect than what remained for them in Vancouver.

On hearing the news, Lisa shoved a butterfly t-shirt, her stuffed armadillo, and her ball glove into a knapsack and declared she was going to her best friend's house to live, while Bobby crawled into his toy chest and refused to come out.

They bought an old church overlooking the sea and Michael moved up early to start the renovations. While he tore away at the crumbling Christian stone of the church's decrepit past, Tanya stayed behind to clean out the house and gather food and supplies, as if packing for an apocalypse. She scrubbed grape stains in rugs, cleared mouldy oranges from under beds, and threw away a dusty sock she found behind the fridge.

Because all their money went into the restaurant, Tanya's parents bought them a piece of land and an Airstream to live in, until they built their house. As Michael tracked down stonemasons, interviewed cooks, entered figures in spreadsheets, and rifled through paint chips,

Tanya and the kids moved into a trailer in a field flush with stinging nettles and blackberry brambles.

For the first few years, the restaurant was packed every night. They turned people away. Then the flurry of excitement and rave reviews faded beneath the flutter and noise from late plates and shabby presentations. Reservations were cancelled. Cooks were fired or quit.

One day before heading into work to face the latest staffing shitstorm, Michael went for a hike in the woods behind the trailer. Following a rough path through the trees, he arrived at a clearing where a patch of sunshine fell on a shack built and abandoned by a hermit artist. A woman's naked torso appeared in the attic window, a splash of light bouncing off her glass-tempered flesh. Another woman walked over and caressed her neck, her shoulder.

A boom echoed in the distance. Michael turned towards the sound. Dynamite. Another logging road being built up the inlet. When he looked back at the window, there was nobody there.

That afternoon, his sous chef, Marnie, said she was going to have to put Travis back on the line.

"Absolutely not. I don't want him touching my plates."

"We don't have anyone else."

"Get someone."

"From where? You've burned through every cook in town."

"I don't care. Fix it. That's your fucking job," Michael yelled, as he stomped into the walk-in cooler and started rearranging boxes of organic lettuce mix.

"I'll try the college again," Marnie said, when he emerged cold and chastened. "You need more halibut?"

"How was the last delivery?"

"Good. Fresh, firm. We should put in another order tomorrow."

"Do it," Michael said, pausing before he turned away. "Thanks."

He pulled into his driveway after work and stopped in front of the huge empty shell that was their home-in-waiting, the truck's headlamps shining a spotlight on the husk of a house that Tanya needed him to finish, that he needed to finish.

He felt the throb of pressure like a steady rain of blows to his chest.

Gazing at the tattered Tyvek flapping in the breeze and the blue plastic tarps covering the unfinished roof, he remembered being ensconced in their tin can trailer with the rain beating down that first winter, when it was all still a big adventure.

He'd coaxed the kids into drawing pictures of their dream house using broken crayons and construction paper.

"If you could have anything in your room, what would it be?" he asked.

"Tigers," said Bobby. "And four hundred puppies."

"How about we paint your room to look like a jungle or we could make racecar shaped bunk beds...?"

"I know, I know," Bobby said, jumping up with his hand held high, as if trying to get the teacher's attention. "An aquarium full of sharks."

"Okay, let's focus on something other than turning your room into a zoo. Can you do that, buddy?"

Bobby slumped in his chair.

"What about you, Lisa?"

"Can I have a floor hockey gym?"

"I gotta hand it to you kids. You're not afraid to think big."

"Wonder where they get that from?" Tanya asked.

"This from the woman wanting a Wolf gas range and Sub-Zero fridge," said Michael, who had his own grand plans.

He envisioned a wing of bedrooms overlooking the ocean, a restaurant-grade kitchen with an outdoor pizza oven, and at the heart of his home, a magnificent fireplace built with stones he'd painstakingly selected from the beach down the road.

What he wanted was a house that was spectacular, a house that would weep architectural wonder. What he had was a warren of hollow rooms strewn with nails, metal flashing, and sawdust. And a large pile of rocks in the middle of the living room floor.

In early spring, he'd been forced to mortgage their land. The restaurant wasn't bringing in enough money and the local building supplier refused to sell him windows until he paid his bill.

He said nothing to Tanya.

No matter how hard he tried, he was thwarted at every turn. The roofer failed to show after Michael stayed home from work to meet him. Twice. Then, when the plumber hung up on him after his fifth call that day to discuss the rock garden waterfall in the master bedroom en-suite, Michael's fury swelled, prickling his skin like a radiation rash.

Still, he waxed eloquent to Tanya about skylights that would open with large metal rods, the way fruit markets roll out their awnings at the start of each day.

"Just get the water hooked up before you start carving holes in our nonexistent roof," she said.

Michael thought being with Tanya would make him a better man. Instead, he felt worse about who he was, and behaved more badly than he intended. She was the decent one. He was the caustic wild man.

From the moment they met working on the line at an upscale restaurant in downtown Vancouver, he'd been impressed by her Zen master vibe. Even during the chaos of restaurant service, she'd worked calmly, quietly, her upper body staying solid and true as she plated dozens of desserts at a breathtaking pace. He was capable of nudging an appetizer from good to great, but equally capable of swiping a mediocre entrée onto the floor in a flash fit of temper, scaring the dishwashers. She admired his reckless creativity and kept him from spinning too far into the ether. At least she used to.

Or maybe he'd stopped paying attention.

FOUR YEARS AFTER leaving Vancouver, they were still living in a trailer in a field full of blackberry bushes, when Michael turned his attention to the land. He became obsessed with growing their own food, with being self-sufficient. They could even supply the restaurant with fresh herbs and vegetables.

Fuck the suppliers with their exorbitant prices and shitty produce.

Using the last of the money he borrowed from the bank, he rented a backhoe to rip out the weeds. He built raised beds that he shored with found lumber, threw up some posts, strung old fishing net around them, and called it a garden.

Once, he would have fussed over every detail, but perfection was a luxury he could no longer afford.

There were still salmon to fillet, waiters to hire, sauces to concoct.

At the house, walls had to be erected, sheets of plywood nailed, metal roofing installed.

Then, the morning after his argument with Marnie, he was gutted to discover that a deer ventured into the garden just as everything had started growing. It left behind a row of lettuce reduced to nubs, fruit trees littered with chewed leaves, and a peppering of hoof prints in the soil.

Michael felt like a glass bottle tossed in the air, waiting to shatter.

He retreated to his shed. After pushing aside scraps of tin roofing propped against the wall, he grasped a bottle of Cutty Sark and took a long swig to tame his raging pulse. Then another. And another. After finishing the bottle, he went outside to patch the hole the deer worried in the fence.

Later that afternoon, he played soccer with Tanya and the kids in the field beside their house. Boys against girls. Lisa was a go-getter. She flew down the field, running and charging and kicking. When the ball came to Bobby, he got distracted and forgot which end was his goal.

Michael put his hands on Bobby's shoulders.

"Okay, kiddo. We need to score," he said, nudging the ball to his son. "Can you kick it between those two cones?"

Bobby nodded.

"Go," Michael said, blocking his daughter with a little more Scotch-stoked force than he'd intended.

"Dad," Lisa protested.

"Now!"

Bobby wound up and whiffed the ball.

"Jesus Christ, boy, what is wrong with you?"

Lisa charged forward, stole the ball from her brother and shot it into the empty goal at the other end of the field. Bobby crumpled to the ground, crying. Tanya scooped him up, nestling him against her chest as Michael ran inside the trailer. He returned with elaborate ice cream sundaes. A well-worn move from his cowed puppy, lick-fest playbook of forgiveness seeking. Lisa and Bobby devoured the excessive mounds of ice cream and syrup while Tanya stared at Michael, shaking her head, wearily.

Turning his back on his family, Michael stormed off on a tantrum tour of the forest. He kicked shattered cedar logs that lay in his path, then climbed over slash and tree debris, and stomped through patches of moss and moist earth, until he came to the shack where he'd seen the naked women in the window. An eagle trilled in the distance as he stumbled towards the decrepit building.

The door opened and two barefoot women in flowing white clothes beckoned him forward. Blonde, ethereal, and distant, they were like Swedish ghosts with perfect posture. He entered the cabin as if entering another realm. The women, its regal wraithlike rulers.

They told him his aura was ragged yellow with hints of red. They prescribed meditation and a therapy of angels.

He was tempted to believe.

He told them his garden was being ruined and they cast a blessing on it. He said nothing about failing restaurants or faltering wives.

And they offered no cure.

Standing in a rustic cabin with the otherworldly lesbians, he felt as if he could finally breathe. He did not have to be their father or their boss. He didn't have to seduce or charm them. And they were going to help him rescue his garden.

If he could save it, he could save everything.

That night, Bobby and Lisa lay in bed waiting for their father to read them a story while he hunkered in the shed designing an elaborate system of slug-proof beds, deterrent sprays, and a welded wire fence.

Like a cartoon coyote treading air off the side of a cliff, he chose action over inertia, but the drop was the same.

Marnie called to tell him they were shorted on their halibut delivery, the garde manger was sick, and one of the suppliers kept leaving messages about unpaid bills. Her words spun out into dead air, captured on a satellite server flying over his head, a message he would not hear.

Empty bottles piled up in the corner. He started drinking earlier and earlier each day, until there was no beginning and no end, only pause and continuance.

"The kids are asleep," Tanya said, walking into the shed. "They waited for you."

"I have to figure out how to protect the garden. The deer are getting in. They'll ruin everything."

"We can't keep this up, Michael."

"I know. But it's close."

"What's close? Nothing is remotely close to what it should be."

"The garden. I just need to build a proper fence."

Tanya looked at the rusty lawn mower in the corner, the lumpy bags of sod and fertilizer, and the clumps of hardware bulging from open drawers beneath the hastily constructed workbench, where her husband sat transfixed by the drawing in front of him.

"Michael."

"Hmmm?"

"You need help."

"No, I've got this. I'll come to bed soon."

An hour later, he passed out in the shed.

In the morning, when he went home, he found Tanya's gumboots lying on the floor beside the couch, Lisa's neon orange t-shirt hanging from a bunk bed railing, and an empty granola box sitting in the sink.

A note was propped against the wooden saltshaker on the kitchen table beside Mr. Socks. Bobby never went anywhere without his stuffed bunny. Michael picked him up, stroking the worn fur of his limp long ears.

He needed to see the lesbians.

He would take them a cake. Normally, he preferred the free-wheeling style of cooking to the rigid rules of baking, but he wanted to do something special for them.

He chased away the emptiness with the clatter of spoons, bowls and pans, seeking solace in puffs of flour and the slip and slide of oozing eggs. The smell of baking butter and roasted nuts reminded him of nestling into Tanya's sleep-warmed flesh and breathing in her earthy morning fragrance. Though he couldn't remember the last time he'd done that.

He peeked in at the browning batter and realized he'd forgotten the salt. In the past, he would have plucked out the offending abomination and thrown it away. This time, he carried the flawed almond cake and a bottle of Cutty Sark into the woods.

But there was no sign of the Swedish lesbians.

He tried to conjure them, as if adjusting the rabbit ears on an old-fashioned TV to make figures reappear from within the static. He thought he caught brief glimpses of their billowing white clothes and heard snatches of their wispy pronouncements, then it all faded inside the crackle of his stuttering synapses.

Inside the cabin, he plopped onto the dusty bench under the window and shovelled handfuls of cake into his mouth. The missing salt made it taste odd. That didn't stop him from eating the entire pan as he stared at the rough lumber walls.

Then, he started in on the Scotch.

After finishing the bottle, he lay down and gazed out the window at the sea of naked tree trunks, their needle-laden branches up high, beyond his fallen vision.

As he drifted off to sleep, he grieved what he refused to believe he'd lost. When he woke, cold, nauseous and drunk, he wandered home only to discover that a deer had eaten his Swiss chard.

The lesbians had abandoned him, and his garden was ruined.

Again.

That's when he got the gun.

He'd bought it the year before, planning to put venison on the menu to accompany the chanterelles, stinging nettles, and wild leeks he would forage. He never picked the mushrooms. Never cooked the nettles. And he never got his hunting license.

He found the rifle in a corner of the shed behind a clump of two-by-fours. He loaded it with cartridges and went back outside. Poking his head into the trailer to see if Tanya had returned, he was startled to find pools of spilled batter, flour-filled footsteps, and a crooked tower of dirty dishes in the sink.

Chefs are trained to clean up after themselves. He'd never left a mess like that before. Unnerved by the state of the kitchen, he ignored Tanya's note as he scooped up Mr. Socks from the kitchen table and retreated to the garden.

Perched on a log near the patched-up hole in the fence, he held Bobby's stuffed bunny on his knee; its little rabbit head drooping forward as if too heavy for its spindly neck.

And he waited.

A coyote called in the distance, an eerie lament of loss and longing as Michael drummed an impatient tattoo on the gun lying in his lap beside his son's favourite toy.

As he sat alone, hiding from the moonlight, his eyes started to droop. His hands went limp, arms falling to his side. He slouched against the tree and fell asleep.

The deer arrived at dawn. Michael jolted awake and fumbled with the rifle. He lifted it to his shoulder, took aim, his muscles tensing as he cocked the hammer. The doe stood frozen against the pink and orange sky, her ears alert, her eyes large and scared. He pressed his index finger against the cold hard metal.

He couldn't do it. He couldn't pull the trigger.

"Go on," he yelled. "Get out of here."

The deer bolted and Mr. Socks fell to the ground. Michael didn't notice. He was too busy knocking down the stupid fence that did not do its job, the fence that was so badly conceived, so shoddily built that it ruined what it was supposed to protect. He pulled it down piece-by-piece, yanking and ripping and tearing, until the garden lay completely exposed.

He picked up the rifle and fired into the mess of webbing on the ground, the shots reverberating against the silence.

Chameleons

EVERY SUMMER for her birthday, Sally got a present she didn't want. One year, it was a trip to Sudbury to see a nine-metre-high version of a five-cent piece. Another time it was a bike, which she did want, but it was an old lady's bike instead of a slick purple one with banana seat, high handlebars, and hand brakes like the one Kelly Mason got for Christmas. The weekend of her fourteenth birthday, her father said he had a surprise. She hoped for a chemistry set but expected the equivalent of a trip to the Big Nickel.

As they drove past the lake that looked like an ocean, she dared to dream though knew she shouldn't. Watching the back of her father's thick, sunburned neck as he pulled into a familiar driveway, Sally felt her hidden hope drop like a book knocked to the floor by a careless elbow.

THE FIRST TIME she and her younger brother Greg came to this house with their father, a woman with a dark shock of hair and flaming lips painted into a smile met them at the door.

"Come in, come in, right up here," she'd said, gesturing impatiently for them to come inside, as if they were stumbling towards the wrong house. "I'm so glad you're here today. Come, I want you to meet my children."

Sally trailed after her father and brother who followed Red Lips into the living room, where a teenage girl with a glossy scowl, black eyeliner, and a short floral mini dress examined her painted fingernails. Beside her, a boy Greg's age sat rigidly staring at his shiny black shoes.

"Sally, Greg, these are my kids, Andy and Jenny," the woman said. "Oh, and my goodness, I haven't even told you my name. I'm Faye. I'm a friend of your father's and please, everyone sit down. I'm going to pop into the kitchen for some cookies and Coke while you all get to know each other. I'll be back in a jiffy."

They'd only stayed an hour that time; Saturday dinners with the Wilsons soon became a regular part of weekly visits with their father. Sally said nothing to her mother. After the roast-chicken-swept-to-the-floor incident when Greg ruined his new shoes running through mud puddles, Sally did not want to see how her mother would react to her ex-husband having a new girlfriend. So, she bought her brother's silence with a second-hand soccer ball and six Thor comic books.

On Sally's birthday weekend, the Wilson house seemed empty when they arrived. Sally's father, Fred, opened the side door and called, "Hello."

"In here."

Faye sat on the couch in the living room, sipping from a tall glass as she turned the pages of a fashion magazine. She lifted her head and smiled at Fred as he entered the room.

Andy clomped down the stairs. "Hey man, where's your stuff?"

"What stuff?" Greg asked.

"Your overnight stuff. You guys are here for the weekend, right?"

"No way."

"Way. C'mon, ya wanna see my car set?"

"Yeah," Greg said, running up the stairs after Andy.

This is it? Sally thought. This is my surprise? Suddenly the oversized silver coin standing proud against the Sudbury sky was looking pretty good.

"You go on up to Jenny's room, sweetie," said Faye. "She's out but she'll be home later."

Sally glared at her father's back as he poured a drink from the decanter, its thick diamond edges glinting in the light. Did he not notice the frosted pink sneer on Jenny's lips every time they visited?

What did he care? He had a drink in his hand and a woman who smiled when he entered the room.

Sally reluctantly went upstairs. On their last visit, she'd overheard Jenny yelling at Faye that she didn't want anyone in her room when she wasn't there. She knocked quietly on Jenny's bedroom door. When there was no answer she stepped inside. After grabbing a book about pyramids from Jenny's desk, she climbed into the window seat overlooking the backyard, where she read until she was called down for dinner.

Jenny always showed up for meals during their visits. Except this time. After everyone was done eating, Faye started to clear the table.

"Leave them, honey," Fred said. "Finish your wine. Sally can do the dishes."

"Fred," Faye said. "That's so sweet, thank you."

Yeah, he's a prince, thought Sally, as she took the stack of dinner plates into the kitchen.

On her way back to Jenny's room, Sally caught a glimpse of her father leaning forward in his chair talking to Faye whose arm was stretched across the back of the couch, her body turned away from him.

"There's no excuse for her not to be here. Your daughter has a serious chip on her shoulder, and you need to be firm with her," he said in a low voice.

"What do you want me to do, Fred?" Faye sighed.

Inside Jenny's room Sally climbed back into the window seat and gazed out at the small creek trickling along the ravine behind the Wilson's yard.

"Oh great, you're here," Jenny said an hour later when she flounced into the room and threw herself onto her bed.

Sally wrapped her arms tightly around her bent knees and stared out at the moon, which appeared bright and round against the deepening blue of the sky.

"I don't know why you have to be here," Jenny said. "I'm sick and tired of everyone busting in on me all the time. Just cause Freddy's her boyfriend, doesn't mean you have to be my friend, you know. I'm not going to be stuck with whatever loser her latest creepoid drags in."

"Maybe I don't want to be here anymore than you want me to be here," Sally burst out. "Did you ever think of that?"

"Well, well, it speaks," Jenny said.

Sally turned away and stared out at the clear night sky.

"I guess I should be grateful you're not Cindy the weird," Jenny continued, as she got off the bed, went over to the cork bulletin board above her desk and adjusted the Sunny Montego Bay postcard thumbtacked to the top right corner.

"Man, she was a piece of work. Every weekend, she brought her whole Barbie universe with her. And she'd babble on, 'Barbie and Ken are going scuba diving. Barbie and Ken are climbing Mt. Everest'. I'm like, maybe somebody could kick Barbie and Ken off the stupid mountain. Here, let me. I was never so glad to see the ass end of someone in my whole life."

Jenny walked around the room touching posters, moving books, kicking a sweater under the bed, as if unable to risk sitting still.

"We've had some real winners through here. This one guy wore these old man shorts, ugly Hawaiian shirts, and sandals. Now, if you had black hair on your toes, would you wear open shoes? I don't think so. Worst of all, he liked to play daddy. Like, just cause he stays overnight a couple of times, suddenly we're one big happy family. Barf."

She threw herself on her bed again as if she'd just finished a cross-country race, then popped back up immediately and announced she was going to sleep. She pulled off her shirt and shorts, slipped on a nightgown, turned out the light and crawled under the covers.

Sally stayed where she was until she heard the steady rhythm of Jenny's sleep breathing. In the corner, away from the streaming moonlight, she changed into her pajamas and slipped into bed beside her. Lying very still, Sally looked out at the small wisps of cloud washing across the sky.

When she woke up, she was alone.

In the kitchen, she found Faye standing at the counter wearing a blue silk kimono with a large black dragon stitched on the back.

"Good morning, honey. Happy birthday. Do you want toast?"

"No, thank you."

Fred sat at the dining room table reading the newspaper. "Happy birthday, kiddo. Sleep well?"

"Uh huh."

The place setting beside her was untouched while the rest of the table was a chaos of crumbs, puddles of milk, and jam-smeared knives lying skewed across vinyl place mats. Faye set a plate of toast beside Fred, turned to Sally and said, "Are you sure you don't want any?"

"Uh uh."

Sally poured herself a bowl of cereal and resting her cheek on her fist, she watched the orange curled flakes floating in milk.

After finishing her breakfast, she wandered outside and found Greg hanging from a tree branch, swinging his legs in the air.

"Come on, man. Do it. Jump," said Andy. "Greggie boy's a chicken... Buck, buck, buck..."

"Shut up. Look out below," Greg hollered as he dropped down in front of them.

"Have you seen Jenny?" Sally asked.

"This is boring," Andy said. "Let's go to the park."

"Andy. Where's your sister?"

"I dunno."

Then they were gone.

Sally walked toward the creek and sat on the bank, hidden away from the house. Lying down beneath the large maple tree, its tangle of limbs shooting off in different directions, she searched for familiar shapes hidden within the clouds drifting across the sky but found nothing she could recognize.

Until a movement on the tree trunk caught her eye. She sat up and stared at a small reptile-like body clinging to the bark. Its long tail quivered with alertness like a garter snake hidden in the grass. Bulging bright globes on either side of its head glistened. Sally watched, fascinated by its stillness, when suddenly it bolted up the tree.

At lunch, Sally said, "I saw this weird lizard thing in the backyard."

Andy punched Greg in the shoulder.

Greg said, "Take off," and punched him back.

"Boys, boys," Faye said fluttering her hands at them.

Jenny rolled her eyes as she breezed into the room, sat down at the table, grabbed a bun, and slathered it with butter.

The boys continued to bat at each other with slaps of affection until Fred said, "That's enough."

Andy reached under the table and pinched Greg's leg, causing Greg to yelp, his fork clattering onto the plate. Fred looked up and when he saw that all was quiet again, he resumed eating.

Sally gazed around the table, but it was as if she was in some bubble where no one could see or hear her. Standing abruptly, she took her plate into the kitchen.

Jenny came in behind her and said, "That thing you saw was probably a chameleon. Did it change colours?"

"No," Sally said, not sure if Jenny was making fun of her.

"You should catch one and put it in with different stuff, like grass and bark. You'll see."

"Girls, can you come in here, please," Faye called.

Jenny held her finger to her pursed lips saying, "Shhh," then slipped out the back door.

"Where's Jenny?" her dad asked when she returned to the dining room.

Sally shrugged. Fred looked over at Faye.

"So, we've got a little something for the birthday girl," Faye said putting a package in front of Sally. "This is from all of us."

Sally tore off the wrapping paper and found a pink case with metal clasps and a lock. Inside were three rows of purple, green and blue eye shadow, a pair of fat tiddlywink-like containers with different shades of creamy red blush, and a fluffy bunny tail covered in perfumed body talc.

"Thanks," she said closing the lid on the makeup her mother would never let her use.

"Can we go to the park now?" Andy asked.

"Yes. But be back by five. We're going out for dinner tonight. It's a special occasion," Fred said.

As Sally left the dining room, she heard her father asking Faye how many more kits she'd have to sell to win the trip to Puerto Vallarta.

Retreating to her spot down by the creek, Sally lay on the grass, getting lost in daydreams about searching for rare birds in the Amazon. When she felt footsteps on the ground behind her, she sat up, the back of her head wet and warm from the ground. Jenny came towards her holding a shoebox, its rust-coloured lid tucked underneath, like when a salesclerk rustles through tissue paper to uncover a pair of fancy new shoes.

Jenny, wearing a starburst yellow blouse, purple plastic sandals and a large straw sunhat, came towards Sally like a miniature movie star strolling past a mob of screaming fans. When she got close, she broke into a run then plopped down on the grass beside Sally, shoving the open box under her nose.

"Look," she said, "I found one. It's not really a chameleon, but that's what we call them cause of how they change colours to blend in. You'll see."

Sally bent closer and saw a pile of dewy sweet-smelling grass with a small green creature, like the one she'd found earlier. She looked up at Jenny, her chest feeling tight and small.

"Okay, now watch this," Jenny said, as she gently lifted the chameleon up and placed it on a piece of bark that was buried beneath the grass. It stood frozen and Sally saw it fade from green to dull brown.

"Amazing. How does it do that?" she asked.

"Dunno. Pretty cool, huh?"

"Yeah."

"And the funny part is he thinks he's safe. It's like he's invisible now. Nothing could hurt him."

The box jiggled as Jenny shifted. The chameleon startled, crawled into a corner and tried to climb out, its colours continuing to darken.

"How come it's getting browner?" Sally asked.

"Probably cause it's afraid."

"We should let it go."

Jenny held the container towards Sally. "Do you want to do it?"

Sally took the box and tipped it towards the ground. The chameleon clambered backwards trying to stay inside. Once the box stopped moving, it scurried out onto the grass, ran up the tree trunk and disappeared into the leaves.

Sally instantly regretted letting it go. She felt a sharp hole gouged into the pit of her stomach.

"What if it stays that colour?" she asked. "It might get eaten."

"It'll change back," Jenny assured her. "And, even if it didn't, at least it won't get stepped on by something that doesn't even see it."

Sally's father called out the back door, telling her to come inside and get cleaned up for dinner.

"Are you coming?" Sally asked Jenny.

"Not a chance."

"Why not?"

"You think it's your birthday dinner, don't you?"

Sally blushed and looked away.

"Nope," said Jenny. "They're going to make this big announcement about getting married."

"What? How do you know?"

"I heard my mom saying they were going to tell us at dinner. That's why I bailed yesterday. Guess it's tonight instead. No way I'm sitting through that," Jenny said, standing up and brushing off her bum. "Hey, I guess that'll make us weekend sisters."

"Sally," her dad yelled. "Get in here."

"Leave her alone," Jenny hollered.

Sally stared at her stunned.

"What? You gotta stand up for yourself. Otherwise, they'll stomp all over you."

When her father called Sally again, she turned towards his voice and started slowly walking back to the house.

"Have fun at dinner. See you next time, sis," said Jenny as she ambled down to the creek.

"Why didn't you come when I called you?" her father asked when she came through the door.

Sally shrugged her shoulders and asked, "Why are we going to a restaurant tonight?"

"I need you to go find your brother and Andy and bring them home."

"Are you getting married?"

"Go find the boys," her father said slowly, emphatically, as if speaking to a slow-witted child.

Sally scowled and put her hands on her hips.

"And I don't want any backtalk," he continued. "Just because Jenny has a smart mouth doesn't mean you can get away with it. Now go."

Sally hung her head and walked out the door as if obeying him. But once outside, she bolted around the side of the house, past the maple tree and through the creek. Her runners were heavy and wet when she leaped back onto dry land. She looked around frantically.

She saw a blur of vibrant colour marching off into the distance, and she ran after her.

Untethered

A STEADY RHYTHM of whooshes broke through the early morning calm.

Lexi went to her living room window and gazed outside where a scattershot army of oversized fire hydrants, belugas, and liquorice and lemon striped bumblebees, swarmed across the sky.

She headed out her front door and followed their flight path towards the field behind her place. One rainbow-striped teardrop balloon passed so close, she could see the bursts of flames shooting into the air and hear the propane burner's exhalations, like the exaggerated breaths of a yoga instructor.

When she reached her backyard, she found a collapsed tangle of fabric hanging from the branches of her tree and a large wicker basket lying on the ground in a bed of broken boughs and scattered leaves.

She walked towards the nylon-draped oak.

"Watch out," her next-door neighbour Stan said, as he charged up to their shared fence. "It could be dangerous. I'll come take a look."

"That's okay."

"I'll be right back," he said.

"Really, it's not necessary," she called out as he clanged away inside his shed. He re-emerged carrying a large stepladder and strode into her yard.

"Did you see anyone?" he asked.

"No, but I just got here."

"The pilot must have taken off. He's gonna be in deep shit for crashing. Those things are expensive," he said, shaking his head. "You need to call the city. Get them to clean this mess up. And you might want to get a lawyer."

"Why would I need a lawyer?"

"So you can sue for damages. Not only for the tree. It could have hit your roof on the way down. Might have hit mine. Think I'll call one too."

Stan set his ladder against the tree.

"Wait."

He stopped and looked at her.

"You're right, I should report it. Which means we better not tamper with the evidence," she said, mustering up some CSI-laced lingo to scare him away from her balloon.

Stan hesitated.

"Just until I can get someone from the city to check it out."

"Well, don't take too long," he admonished, reluctantly folding up his ladder. "The whole thing could come down any minute."

Lexi assured him she'd get right on it.

Instead, she searched the Internet for everything she could find about hot air balloons. She learned that once they're set loose, they're completely at the mercy of the wind. Pilots can raise or lower them by controlling the temperature within the envelope, but they cannot choose their path or change direction at will. And they cannot return to the place where they started.

Lexi had almost gone on a hot air balloon safari over the Serengeti after university. In the way that she'd almost volunteered for an international aid organization. Which is to say, she'd picked up a brochure at a career fair and tried to envision being the kind of a person who could dig wells in a Kenyan village, then reward herself by rising above the African savannah in a woven willow basket. It would have been a wonderfully dramatic way to conquer her fear of heights.

Back when conquering her fears seemed like something she might do.

Lexi never did travel overseas. After graduating, she took an entry-level receptionist job at the university and worked her way up to assistant to the dean of the medical school. And now she lived beside a man whose idea of doing good was to foist weed killer on her to rid her lawn of dandelions. She did not want the poison. She had no intention of using it. But she smiled and took the toxic box, then made him blueberry muffins as a thank you.

Lexi wrenched herself away from the rabbit hole of hot air balloon websites, videos, and Pinterest pages into which she'd tumbled, and went outside. She edged towards the tree where the balloon hung stranded and limp, until a sharp rustle of material above her head sent her scurrying backwards, afraid of being buried beneath the plunging remains.

Out of the corner of her eye, she caught a glimpse of a fuzzy faded green object. Misty's favourite tennis ball, the one Lexi always brought along for their Saturday afternoon walks in the woods, lay on the edge of the flowerbed. She picked it up and swept bits of soil off it, then plopped down on the grass, letting the ball fall to the ground. She rubbed her eyes with her fists and tried not to cry.

When she heard Stan's screen door slam, she hurried back inside. She couldn't face him. Not now.

Once she dared to dream of a cottage by the ocean with a mango garden and a wraparound deck. What she had was a semi-detached house next to a retired Radio Shack manager in a gritty neighbourhood bordering a rough cluster of streets in a landlocked Ontario town.

Her first encounter with Stan was early one morning soon after she'd moved in. She'd been quietly reading with Misty lying at her feet, revelling in the silence before the snow blowers began warming up like an orchestra in training, when she was startled by the sound of a loud cough.

Lexi was shocked to realize that the only thing separating her from her neighbour was a wall that let every sound seep through, as if there was nothing more than a worn sheet hanging between their lives.

The next day, Stan appeared at her door bearing a book of leftover coupons from a local charity fundraiser, after the good ones had been picked out. He suggested they exchange numbers. Just for emergencies. The following week he phoned to tell her to call the city about the sloppy snow clearing on their street. They only responded if everyone did it.

Over the coming months, he offered to show her how to paint her porch, trim her hedge, and spray-wash her driveway. If she didn't want to do the work herself, she could hire his son who did odd jobs around Stan's place. When she failed to take him up on his offers, Stan's suggestions morphed into overt complaints. Her dog barked too much. Her elm was dead and should be taken down.

She came home from work one day to find the tree in her front yard gone. She knew Stan was responsible. He must have the city's complaint line on speed-dial and called to claim her elm was dangerous. She was tempted to confront him. But Lexi did not do confrontation. She was an appeaser, not a disrupter.

Her sister always dabbled in bad behaviour without suffering the consequences. Lexi tried smoking in the girls' washroom in high school once and was not only caught and reprimanded publicly in front of a squad of cool girls, she was also kicked off the yearbook committee. The committee she'd only joined to be close to Pablo. When she could no longer spend time with the boy she'd had a crush on since grade 9, she started skipping class and almost flunked out.

That was the kind of warning they should put on cigarette packages to keep teenage girls from smoking.

THE NIGHT AFTER the balloon crashed into her tree, Lexi couldn't sleep. She wandered around the house checking for leaky water taps and other signs of impending disaster. She'd been doing these late-night inspections more and more since putting Misty down.

Once the cancer spread to her brain, there was nothing that could be done. Lexi had been in the room with her at the end, her hand pressed against her dying dog's side as the needle took effect, the ache in her stomach sharpening as Misty's breathing slowed and then stopped.

A month later, Lexi still felt untethered.

Wide-awake in the early morning hours, she sat at the kitchen table with a cup of chamomile tea listening to the tick-tock of the sun-shaped clock hanging on the wall above the sink. An odd noise came from next door. Tilting her head towards the sound, she followed the subtle scritch scratch as it moved back and forth, and up and down, like a tiny mouse with sharpened toenails chasing a shifting shadow.

It creeped her out. Because she didn't know what it was. Because it was sneaking around her house in the middle of the night.

It had to be Stan. It was always Stan. Even when she couldn't hear him, she sensed him next door, rattling around in his mirror version of her house. Proximity and shoddy building practices forced them into an intimacy she'd never wanted. Now, she felt like she couldn't get away from him. Even when she went onto her back deck, he'd be poking around on the other side of the fence.

Digging? Planting?

Burying a body?

Lexi finally fell asleep, only to be woken by the doorbell. Her first thought was that it was someone coming for the balloon. She didn't want them to take it.

Not yet.

An officious looking man stood on her front step with a clipboard and pen.

"Ms Anderson?"

"Yes."

"Do you own a dog?"

"What?"

After the man left, Lexi went upstairs. She looked out over the backyard, at the mess in her tree, at the storm clouds moving in from the direction the balloons had come the day before. She wondered what happened to the pilot. Did they crawl out and make their escape? Were they coming back to rescue their balloon?

Tiny electric shocks cascaded down Lexi's arms as a car with a loud throaty muffler pulled into the driveway next door. She shook out the prickling in her hands, returned to her bedroom and peeked out the front window.

Stan's son stepped out of his low-slung red Camaro and walked across his father's front lawn like an amped up bodybuilder whose muscles had overwhelmed his frame. He grabbed some tools and a bucket from the shed, headed to the lilac bush and spread fertilizer around it. Then he pruned the branches, creating a small bouquet from the trimmings, which he wrapped in a wet paper towel and placed in the backseat of his car. There was no sign of Stan.

As the sickly-sweet stench of bruised lilacs wafted through the air, churning her stomach, Lexi could no longer ignore the beginnings of a migraine. The tingling in her fingers, the faint throbbing at the base of her skull. If Misty were there, she'd be sticking close, nudging her hand, pressing against her leg. She seemed to know before Lexi did when one was on its way. And the warmth of Misty's body against her side as she lay in a dark room after the migraine's force slammed her down could dull the raging pain, edging it closer to bearable.

Lexi swallowed one of her migraine pills, then closed her window and shut the curtains. She lay down, hoping to sink beneath the worst waves of misery like a scuba diver slipping into the ocean to escape the seasickness that only strikes at its surface. As the medication muffled the stabbing at her temples, she drifted off to sleep.

For the second time that day, she was woken by the doorbell. She staggered out of her room, her brain fuzzy and thick from the drugs and a migraine hangover and opened her front door to find Stan on the stoop.

"I thought you were the bylaw officer coming back," Lexi said, rubbing her forehead.

"Oh? Was he here about the balloon?"

"No," she replied, glaring up at him through the faint lines still zigzagging across her vision. "He was here about my dead dog."

Stan looked away.

"Figures," he blustered. "Typical bureaucratic efficiency. Showing up months after the fact. Since presumably your dog was alive when the complaint was lodged."

"Presumably."

"Anyway," he said, holding out a business card. "Here's the number of a lawyer I know. For when you go after the city."

Lexi saw that his son's car was gone from the driveway. The only sign that he'd been there was the freshly moistened soil around the base of the lilac bush. She realized she'd never seen Stan and his son together.

"I'm not going to sue anyone," Lexi said, looking at Stan's outstretched hand, at the scraped knuckles and the tiny flecks of paint spattered across his fingers. She thought about sandpaper and drywall and those sounds in the middle of the night.

"You might want to rethink that, young lady. The city is clearly at fault for letting that ridiculous hot air balloon festival go ahead."

Lexi crossed her arms and stared at him.

"Suit yourself," Stan said, shrugging.

Black clouds formed in the sky over his shoulder.

"Yes, I think I will," she replied, retreating into her house.

After that, the storm moved in quickly and settled hard. Lexi watched the torrents of rain come down, puddles growing and spreading until they encroached on front lawns all along the street.

How sad does a man have to be to call a cop on a dog?

Stan would keep railing against life's inconveniences, sucking her into his slipstream if she let him. No wonder his son came when he was away.

Lexi went downstairs to gather Misty's doggie bed, leash, and snowman-shaped rubber Kong from the furnace room where she'd stowed everything after she'd returned from the vet's office, alone.

She carried the box of paraphernalia upstairs and set it by the front door. In the morning, she would donate everything to the animal shelter. To spare any future pets she might have from the inheritance of her dead dog's past.

As day slipped into night, Lexi retreated to the back of the house and sat cross-legged on the floor in front of the full-length patio doors. She searched for the tattered remnants of the balloon in her tree, the bright colours barely visible in the blowing rain. Even when she lost sight of it, she found comfort in knowing it was there.

Her doorbell rang. But she ignored it.

She lay back on the floor and watched the stubbornly clinging nylon thrash against the storm, while above her, thunder and lightning duelled, a cosmic call and response played out against a black and flash-soaked sky.

Tomorrow she could be kind to Stan.

Dead Reckoning

"LOSE THE PLANE," Bonnie said.

She'd suggested as much before but there was no longer a hint of a hint in the demand.

Bonnie didn't fly. She'd never been inside Al's plane. She wanted him to sell it and buy an RV so they could visit her sister in Kamloops.

Al loved his Otter. He barely tolerated Bonnie's sister, a high school English teacher with pretensions and a red Miata. Most weekends he took the float plane out alone. He'd fly up Queen Charlotte Strait, Vancouver Island to his left, the green mainland mountains appearing off the edge of his wings to the right.

He'd made hundreds of trips over these inlets and islands during the high-flying years. All those flush stranded souls in logging camps with nowhere to spend their money. And the fishing grounds bulged with cash buyers, so there was an ocean full of guys with wads of bills, ready to buy anything to get them through the long, hard days. Weed, speed and coke were the core of his business but there was also a small steady market for heroin.

Up to that point, Al's life consisted of tiny potholes of gain and loss, rather than the gaping canyons of failure or success. It would have taken a special effort not to get rich, after chance dropped him inside that stream of easy flowing cash.

By the time the big money days faded in 1997, he had gone legit. He lived in a mortgage-free house on the beach, and owned Flicks and Flakes, a local video/convenience store. He was a member of the Chamber of Commerce, a tax paying, Conservative-voting, Kiwanis-belonging, all-round regular guy. He'd become respectable, but not so respectable his past could come back and bite him on the ass. No running for mayor or the school board, but moderately competent businessman he could get away with.

He was on his second marriage. His son from the first was a husky, hunting, survivalist mechanic in the Interior. Al didn't have much contact with Jack. Sometimes he thought about him, mostly he didn't.

Al hadn't seen his ex-wife Marlene in over fifteen years. It always surprised him when he thought of her, a slow seep of desire and hazy happiness sneaking up on him, the way drunkenness did. He knew he was romanticizing the past, making it look prettier from a distance than it was up close. But pretty was pretty whether it was close or not, whether it was real or not, and it made him feel good to think of her, though he wished it didn't.

It was Marlene who talked him into the tattoo.

They were in Vancouver after herring season and decided to have a little fun, just the two of them, before picking up Jack who was staying with his grandma in Surrey. After drinking all night in a downtown hotel, they stumbled out onto Granville Street looking for coffee and eggs. Drunk and distracted by the glare of a rare sunny day, Al let Marlene push him into a dark storefront wedged between The Leather Palace and a porn-laced magazine stand.

He slumped in a black vinyl chair, while she looked through pages of testosterone-reeking jaguars and eagles and snakes. His head hurt so much, he only glanced at the design she picked out, barely noticing the needle pulsing against his skin. It wasn't till the next day that he saw the sunset flecked mountain and Soldier of Love, etched on his arm. He was right pissed.

Then, after another round of tequila and cocaine, he and Marlene had a wild night with a rope, handcuffs, and ben wa balls, during which she called him her Soldier of Love. From then on, it reminded him of that time. And he liked that.

Especially since, two years later, she up and disappeared with Jack. She called Al from Saskatoon, said she was sorry, she'd had to move on, did he understand? She honoured his vision, she said, but she needed to find her own path. People talked like that then. Some people did. Al never had. He'd learned to nod and look serious, which he did, sitting alone in his living room, as his wife talked at him from a phone booth on the Prairies. Try to love yourself, Al, Marlene said. Then she hung up.

Five years later, he received a letter from her saying that she was marrying a guy named Bruce and they were living in Scarborough. She said she was sorry to have kept Jack from him all these years, but she'd needed a clean break, and Al needed to sort out his life before he could be a proper father to his son. Al sent her a case of El Tesoro Paradiso Tequila and a painting of Barkley Sound at dusk by an artist she'd always admired.

He got a note from his son that began, Dear Dad. How are you? I am fine. Al asked about Marlene in the letter he sent to his son along with a folded hundred-dollar bill. Jack never spoke of her when he wrote back. Over time, Al's letters grew briefer, then settled into blank pieces of paper wrapped around money, until even those stopped.

Al didn't find out that his son had moved back to BC until Jack called him late one night from a bar in Kelowna and started ranting about hippies and homos and his fuckstick stepfather.

That summer, Al drove to the Okanagan Valley to see his son. He took him out for beer and sirloins. They drank Extra Old Stock and talked about engines and the weather, which was unseasonably cool that year.

Jack invited Al back to his place. They could go hunting in the morning, and then he'd take Al to see his bunker in Osoyoos. It was kitted out with enough to survive for two years when everything went to hell. And it would. Soon. According to Jack.

Al told him he'd better keep moving, he had a meeting to get to in Calgary. But instead of continuing east, he turned back towards the coast, and pulled into a motel just outside Kelowna. Al had no desire to stay with his son, yet he wasn't quite ready to leave him. He spent the night lying on top of the bed, the steady whine of transport trucks barrelling past his window and the intermittent flash of headlights on the ceiling, lulling him into a fitful sleep.

Soon after returning home, Al met Bonnie, a nurse who left the city hoping to save her son, Brad. Six months after they were married, Brad overdosed on heroin. Bonnie was on duty when they brought him in.

She never went back to work after seeing her son wheeled down the hospital hallway on a squeaking gurney that late August night. As far as Al knew, she never went near the hospital again. Mostly, she cooked. He came home to counters laden with loaves of bread and cupcakes and muffins, more than they would ever be able to eat.

Al sometimes took the baked goods to give to his employees at the store. Though usually they sat in his truck and got stale, until sweating guilt, he shoved the hardened food into the garbage can in front of the IGA. Whatever he took was replaced by the time he got back from work.

One day, he didn't take anything with him, and when he came home, the counter was empty. She had done no cooking at all. They went out for dinner. Al thought this was great. Until it happened the next night and the one after that. When he asked her about it, she said she thought he hated her cooking. He assured her that was not true, he missed it terribly.

The next day she made supper. Chicken casserole with string beans and cherry pie for dessert. Not too much. Not too little. Finally, things were just right.

Then Bonnie found God.

She did not join a congregation or seek shelter inside a church, synagogue, or mosque. Her God was personal, demanding, and harsh. Each evening Al came home to find the bible opened to a new page and he soon grew accustomed to the acrid smell of a burning candle illuminating the passage of the day. It seemed a familiar story, epistles and singed wax, but he couldn't remember the tale it told.

At first, he looked the passages over, thinking she was leaving him some kind of message, and after reading one too many sentences about smiting this and smiting that, he figured that if she was trying to tell him something, he'd just as soon not know what it was.

Al didn't mind Bonnie spending her time chasing the holy. He did mind when she expected him to do the same.

"Why don't we watch the Ten Commandments again, tonight," she said one evening at supper.

"Can't. I'm meeting Murray for a drink."

"Oh," she said, picking up the dinner plates and taking them to the sink. "I thought you were going to spend more time at home."

"It's just one night."

Al heard the sharp sound of metal clinking on glass, as Bonnie scraped the leftover food into the garbage.

"Besides," he said, pushing his chair away from the table. "It'll be good to go out with the boys. It's been awhile since I had some fun."

Bonnie said nothing, but the dark hurt look she gave him when he left, lingered in the back of his mind, as he pushed open the wooden door of the bar.

The Tankard felt dirty even after it was cleaned, smelling damp and earthy, no matter how sunny it was outside. This was a bar that nobody could make look good and Al liked that about it.

He was on his third pint, in the middle of a heated debate on the merits of Murray's new Ford F-150, which Al thought was a big piece of shit, being a Chevy man through and through, when the phone rang. Lucy, the bartender, hollered to Al that the wife was on the phone. Al continued telling his story about the Chevy he'd bought when he was seventeen, how he'd finally taken a sledgehammer to it, or the damn thing would never have stopped running.

"Chevys will go forever if you let them," he said, walking towards the bar. "Fords don't rust cause they're never out of the shop long enough to sit in the rain."

"Bullshit," Murray flung at his back as Al picked up the phone.

"Hi honey, I was wondering when you're coming home."

"Jesus. I don't know. I'm just having a couple of drinks."

"I wish you wouldn't take the Lord's name in vain, Al. Please don't stay out late."

He thought he'd wiped the call from his mind, and, an hour later when the phone rang, Al looked up. He knew it was for him.

"I fell down the stairs," Bonnie said. "I twisted my knee but I'm okay."

Al finished his beer and left the bar. He found Bonnie sitting in the dark. "I was afraid to try the stairs on my own," she said.

"Alright, I'm here now. Let's get you off to bed."

Bonnie stood up, faltering slightly as she put her weight on her injured knee. Al stepped forward to steady her. Wrapping his arm around her waist, he helped her up to the bedroom. After he got her settled, he returned to the living room and sat on the couch looking out onto the quiet street. He had another couple of drinks then went to bed.

Lying awake for hours with beer floating through his system and Bonnie's arm heavy across his chest, Al's thoughts slammed into one another like a mess of bumper cars driven by ten-year-old kids. Weigh bills and payroll. Candles and guilt. Beer and bravado and grown-up boys. Mini moments flaring and fading until he remembered that time he'd almost crashed into a mountain.

It was soon after he'd started flying. He was casing out the fishing grounds for a plant that hired him to track the sockeye stock. He'd travelled further north than usual and was caught by a fog that blew in thick and fast. Most of the time, he could still make out the water below.

But not always.

The drone of the engine faded as he became enveloped in a blanket of haze. His mind taut with tension, he'd watched for an opening. Then it happened. A gap in the mist. Straight ahead, a dark wall of green where it shouldn't be. He pulled hard to the left, towards what he hoped was open sea.

He descended from the clouds safely that summer morning, and he never again came so close to flying bold and free. And he missed that feeling, that fresh air gust of danger and possibility.

Like he missed Marlene but shouldn't.

Like he wanted to miss Jack but didn't. Maybe if he'd spent more time with him, he wouldn't be so baffled by a son who spent his weekends at an underground shelter in Osoyoos with a bunch of gun-toting preppers, waiting for the end of the world. Who the hell was he to question Jack's life? Military drills and survivalist training might well be the perfect antidote to a childhood spent with stoned hippie parents who seemed surprised they had a child, whenever he walked into the room.

When he bought his Otter, back before Bonnie, before Jack and Marlene, Al was able to go where he wanted, when he wanted. And what had he done with that freedom? Sweet fuck all. He'd been nothing but a petty drug dealer flying up and down the coast in a bush plane.

He could pretend that he might have done more, that he could have been more, if not for the weight of obligation and plain bad luck. The truth was, he was careless with his life. He let things slip through his fingers, then mourned what fell away.

When Jack was a boy, Al bought some land up the sound to build a fly-in fishing lodge. He'd done nothing with it, beyond putting in a dock and slapping up a storage shed. Then, last year a fire swept through. A week later when he flew over, smoke still swirled from smouldering bits of wood and ash, and seared tree trunks dotted the blackened forest floor.

Al slipped out of bed without waking Bonnie. He went downstairs and lit the wood stove to take off the early morning chill. Maybe it was time to visit the land again. He'd take Bonnie. They could pick mushrooms. Morels did well after a forest fire.

Because she refused to fly, Al borrowed a buddy's boat to run them up the inlet. The faint smell of charred cedar lingered in the air. Or maybe he was imagining it as they stepped out onto the dock, which was singed but otherwise intact. The air was deathly quiet. Most of the wildlife fled the flames and did not return. Bonnie bowed her head in front of the ravaged land and prayed, while Al stood with his hands in his pockets, and looked out over the ruins.

He'd never talked much about his past to Bonnie. She assumed he made his money fishing.

After her son died, he was glad he'd let her hold on to that belief.

He would let her hold on to all her beliefs.

But he was keeping the plane.

Bonnie wandered across the burnt land, rooting through mounds of earth, gathering the morels that poked up from the soil. All around them, clumps of light brown honeycomb fungi erupted from the damaged earth, alongside the wispy purple petals of rampant fireweed. They picked twenty pounds of mushrooms before taking a break to eat chicken sandwiches that tasted of cooler.

"Pretty good haul," Bonnie said. "I'll use some in a pasta for dinner tonight. We can dry the rest. They'll be nice to have over the winter. "

"Sounds good."

"Too bad you never built the lodge. Though it would have been hard to see it wiped out by fire," she said. "Still, it's never too late."

"Maybe."

Al folded the wax paper from his sandwich, put it back into the cooler, and grabbed a beer. "It's probably too late," he said.

"Not if you sell the plane," she said, tossing the last bit of her sandwich into the water.

Al turned away and walked across the scorched earth. He headed up the hill at the back of his property. At the top, he could see straight up the sound. In the other direction was the protected bay where Bonnie sat staring at the water. She believed he was selling the plane.

Bonnie had always believed. So did Jack and Marlene. It didn't matter much what they believed, just that they did.

Cottage Country

KIMMY LAY ON the living room couch while marching band music blasted from old crackling speakers. Her younger sisters slept on a pullout bed in the spare room while her dad, Phil, drank in the kitchen with his friend, Chuck, a bus-driving bachelor with a steep love of rye and Coke.

"No way I'm putting up with that shit," Phil said.

"Unbelievable."

Kimmy burrowed into the bulging cushions of her makeshift bed, squinched her eyes shut, and covered her ears. A slurry of words leaked through the cymbals and big bass drums.

"I'm a good guy," said Phil.

"Sure, you are."

"You don't see me walking away from my kids. Not like that bastard who up and left us like we were spoiled meat."

"Your old man was bad news," said Chuck. "Not you. You're one of the good ones."

A loud banging interrupted them. They went silent, the clash of percussion peppering the air.

"I know you're in there," yelled Phil's wife, Mandy, from out in the hallway. "Open up."

Kimmy uncovered her ears and lay rigid on her back.

Mandy screamed, "Do you hear me?" She kicked the apartment door. "Why don't you tell your precious daughters what you did to me, you bastard."

"Knock it off," Phil growled. "Or I'll really give you something to complain about."

"I've already got plenty to complain about, asshole."

"I mean it. Get the hell out of here."

"Where am I supposed to go?" she cried.

There was a scraping sound, then the low rumble of Phil's voice followed by more yelling. The click and swoosh of locks and chains released. Frantic whispers, a scuffle, bodies clashing, a bang against the door.

Then silence.

Kimmy pulled the covers up over her head and lay still in the dark, her breath moist and heavy against the wool blanket.

The next morning, when she woke to find her father sitting in an armchair reading the paper, she wondered if she had dreamt it all. After her dad went to take a shower, she opened the apartment door and saw a black scuffmark at the bottom of the hallway side of the door.

She looked down the dark orange and brown hallway as if expecting to find Mandy stepping into the creaking elevator on her way to some other life, all she saw was an empty corridor of beige broadloom and foil flecked wallpaper. Kimmy closed the apartment door just as her father came back into the living room smoothing his wet hair and smelling of Old Spice.

Lola walked into the kitchen. "Where's Mandy?"

"She's not here."

"Where is she?" Lola asked.

"Never mind," their father said. "Kimmy, I want you to go to the store for some milk. And take your sister with you."

"I wanna go too," said Fran, shuffling into the living room in her pyjamas.

In the elevator, Kimmy said, "She's not coming back."

"How do you know?" Lola asked.

Kimmy shrugged.

"But where did she go?"

KIMMY DIDN'T CARE that Mandy was gone. She no longer believed in Santa or the Tooth Fairy. And she no longer believed in her father's women. Not his last one, the brittle real estate agent who drank whisky neat and talked fast and forever, like an express train barrelling through the Prairies. Or the one before that, a tall, fragile widow who lounged on a settee smoking Benson and Hedges like a bruised beauty in a black and white movie, waiting to shoot her cheating man.

Mandy was supposed to be different. For one thing, Phil married her. Kimmy and her sisters were flower girls at their wedding. The bride, her spun sugar hair piled atop her head, followed her new stepdaughters down the aisle as they strewed petals along the carpet, Fran occasionally flinging fistfuls of flower parts to the floor in a burst of enthusiasm.

Later, at the reception in a hotel conference room, Kimmy gobbled tiny meringue desserts while Lola, who always gravitated to Phil's girlfriends, grasped Mandy's hand, gazing up at her in naked adoration, basking in her warmth and flowery aroma. Phil tapped his cigarette on a metal ashtray stamped with the hotel's logo, looking pleased and trying not to show it, as he gazed at Mandy aglitter in gossamer and joy.

Kimmy watched as Mandy, her eyes bright and hopeful, searched the room for her new husband. But he turned his back to her, ordering another drink from the bar. Mandy squeezed Lola's hand and smiled down at her as Kimmy lingered by the door, crushing a petit four in her fist.

EVERY WEEKEND, Kimmy and her sisters travelled by streetcar from their mother's dilapidated townhouse to the shiny glass and perfect foyer of their father's security-guarded condo. Kimmy found it disorienting to leave the dark, cramped rooms at home and arrive at a high-rise in Etobicoke with a swimming pool and exercise room in the basement.

Her dad's apartment reminded her of the hotels they stayed in on their recent drive to the East Coast. All those bland bare rooms with crappy carpets and ugly drapes. The best part of that trip had been the plates of fried clams she ordered every time they spied the familiar orange roof of a Howard Johnson's.

Along with their regular weekend visits to his condo and the occasional road trip, Kimmy and her sisters spent three weeks with their father at the cottage he rented every year in a small beach enclave on Georgian Bay. The rustic, old-school bungalow with fake wood panels and ratty, stained furniture sat at the end of a narrow dirt road, past the gaudy mini-mansions and ostentatiously modest abodes of the super wealthy.

That is where Kimmy last saw Mandy. Two weeks before she showed up banging on Phil's apartment door.

The skies were bright and clear that summer. Lola and Fran swarming with the other kids like a murmuration of starlings, happy to frolic on the beach, racing in and out of the sun-warmed water. All those rushing rambunctious kids hunting down Pop Tarts, beach towels and lemonade, the creamy tang of Coppertone mingling with the smells of wet bathing suits and toast, and gritty remnants of damp sand falling from their feet onto the cottage floor.

At times, Kimmy dashed forward boldly, impetuously, like the teenager she'd become. Other times, she retreated into the blissful bubble of childhood, to the time when it was easier to gloss over the differences between her life and the lives of the cottage kids. Like the fact that she was pretty sure none of them shopped for back-to-school clothes at a sketchy strip mall in the suburbs or had to contend with the glares of grocery store cashiers, as their mother sorted through a stack of expired coupons.

Which made her crush on Ashley a very bad idea.

Ashley was cottage royalty. Blonde, pretty, and achingly nice, she had the casual confidence of those born into a life of comfort. Unlike some of the snobby cottage kids who stuck to their own, lolling on private beaches and playing tennis with perfect serves and careless backhands, she volunteered at the local summer camp, and wasn't afraid to hang with the common people.

One day Ashley was nursing an Orange Crush on the picnic bench in front of the local burger stand and convenience store, when she invited Kimmy to join her. Immediately smitten by Ashley's mix of shyness and self-possession, the overbite she hid behind her hand when she laughed, and the faint scar above her left eye, which she did not try to conceal, Kimmy felt the skin on her arms prickle.

From then on, she would walk past the store a couple of times a day, hoping to find her there. When she wasn't desperately seeking Ashley, Kimmy hung around the beach in front of her dad's place or wandered the narrow, gravel streets, waiting for something to happen.

The hazy, lazy days melted into one another, meals a haphazard affair thrown together by Mandy between bouts of cocktails, bridge, and beach darts. The appearance of sporadic culinary offerings seldom aligned with the hunger rhythms of children running, tumbling, and splashing their hours away, so the kids frequently resorted to foraging the fridge or scrounging coins to buy candy at the corner store.

Each found their way to get by. Lola had a gift for hanging around kids whose moms were most likely to invite her to dinner. Fran learned to ride Lola's slipstream to a string of cadged meals, while Kimmy gorged on BBQ chips, cheese, and gherkins.

"Wouldn't it be nice to try that new restaurant in town sometime?" Mandy asked one afternoon, as she and Phil sat on the beach. Kimmy lay on a blanket nearby, reading, as the girls played in the water.

"Why don't we just have the shrimp for dinner?" Phil asked.

"There isn't any left."

"Where the hell did it all go?"

"I don't know," Mandy said. "The kids?"

"They can eat hot dogs."

"I didn't eat any of your stupid shrimp," said Kimmy.

"Of course, you didn't," Mandy said, glaring at her.

"Grab me a beer, will you?" Phil said.

Mandy turned sharply towards him, he was busy watching a guy pull his boat up onto the beach. Sighing, she went into the cottage.

Kimmy stood up, walked into the water, and headed towards the horizon. No matter how far she went, the water did not get any deeper. Everything stayed the same; the ridges, like wet sandy speed bumps on the tender soles of her feet, and the splash of water on her shins, as she thrust her legs forward, over and over again.

At the cottage, the kids were let loose like dogs unleashed, to roam as they liked.

Kimmy didn't always know what to do with her freedom. Standing out in the middle of the bay, she looked behind her at the tiny figures in lawn chairs slathering on suntan lotion and drinking afternoon beers, and she knew nobody would notice if the ground dropped off and she went in over her head.

She turned back towards the distant bodies scattered along the beach.

The night before Kimmy and her sisters returned home, Phil invited everyone over for an end of the season blowout. All summer she'd watched the adults get bold and sloppy, pumped up on the bravado gluttonies of Scotch and grilled steak. She didn't need to go through that again.

When her dad's back was turned, she stole a mickey of lemon gin and a can of Fresca from the kitchen and went to the burger stand, where she found Ashley sitting with a couple of other kids she knew by sight.

Ashley had never been anything but unfailingly nice to Kimmy. And Kimmy had never been anything but completely infatuated with Ashley. She was the first flawed beauty Kimmy fell for, and she would not be the last. Because Kimmy, like her father, was sincere but fickle.

In the coming years, she would stumble through a chattering series of broken loves, like a suitcase bumping down a set of stairs. Lola's future included an endless series of hasty decisions and flamboyant flameouts, while baby Fran would have no problem finding a man to soothe the solar flares of her heart.

Kimmy slid into the seat with the cottage kids, poured a glass of gin and Fresca, and offered it to Ashley, who politely declined. Kimmy quickly swallowed the drink and poured another, as the others chatted about school and courses and teachers that she would never know.

Then, as if responding to some secret unseen signal, the group rose as one and strolled down one of the cottage-congested laneways. Kimmy tagged along, carrying her third spiked drink, trying not to slosh it on her shoes, as she walked in the slow, deliberate manner of the amateur drunk.

When she knelt to tie her shoelace, the others carried on, unaware she had stopped. She stood up and followed in their wake as they ambled on without her, the space where she had been swallowed like the surface of a lake closing over a skipping stone that's sunk to the bottom.

Kimmy veered off from the group and turned down one of the sandy paths that led to the water's edge. She took off her shoes and walked barefoot in the cooling sand, the sun slipping away in the distance. She meandered past the plastic lawn chairs, abandoned foam noodles, and sandcastles littering the front yards of cottages looming large against the sky, the dimpled sand, pocked like peanut shells from dozens of playful feet.

She dropped to the ground and hugged her knees to her chest, as lamps came on in cottages around the bay, and bonfires on the beach sent sparks into the darkening sky.

She shut her eyes and felt woozy. Opening them again, the sky appeared to be melting into the barely visible horizon as low-lying clouds were mirrored on the smooth pink and blue sheen of the water's surface and anchored boats, like stationary water bugs, floated atop its calmness.

She turned from the light dappled water, and following the blast of Herb Alpert's trumpet, she headed back towards the cottage, tiny shell-like stones digging into the tender skin of her bare feet as she drew closer. Slipping past her father who was talking to their next-door neighbour, a divorced mom of two boys, she wove her way through the laughing adults, the air thick with the cool fumes of menthol cigarettes.

Kimmy entered the kitchen and snatched a wine cooler. She hid the bottle behind her back and snuck sips on the fly when she thought no one was looking. There were plenty of parties over the summer, the threat of returning to regular life brought an extra charge to the adults' conversations, an intensity to their full-frontal drunkenness.

One of her dad's skeevy friends placed his hand against the wall beside her and complimented her hair, grinning at her like she was a prize he expected to win. She ducked away and edged towards the living room where she saw Mandy sucking hard on a cigarette as she stared out into the night, oblivious to the couple beside her who were bent forward, intent on a private conversation.

Mandy glanced up at Kimmy.

"What are you staring at?" she asked loudly. "You think you're better than me? Honey, you have no idea…"

The woman beside Mandy put a hand on her forearm.

"What?" she turned on the woman, shaking her hand off. "I'm allowed to talk. Don't tell me to settle down."

Mandy stood up and waved her drink, slopping gin and tonic over her hand. "What is wrong with you people?" she asked, her voice cracking as she started to cry.

Frightened by the rawness of Mandy's emotions, Kimmy slipped away from the crowd and hid in the hallway. Peeking around the corner, she watched her father storm into the room, grab Mandy roughly by the arm, and march her outside.

Kimmy set her unfinished cooler on the floor and crept into the room she shared with her sisters. Holding onto the bunk bed ladder, she climbed the rungs unsteadily, her body swaying, as she fought to stay upright. She dove onto the bed and crawled up to her pillow, a bout of the whirlies flaring up until finally, the dizziness settled into a gentle wave undulating in the darkness. Closing her eyes, she drifted off to sleep against a backdrop of querulous voices and desperate laughter, as Paul Simon sang about Kodachrome making him believe all the world's a sunny day.

When she woke the next morning, the cabin was quiet. In the living room she found cigarette butts floating in murky glasses, overturned liquor bottles, and a pair of bikini bottoms lying on the floor.

Lola and Fran were playing outside in the sand, while her dad sat in a lawn chair facing the water. Fighting down swells of nausea, she sat at the table nibbling dry granola.

Mandy walked stiffly into the room. Ignoring Kimmy, she gathered the dirty cups and brimming ashtrays, then grabbing a broom, she began sweeping up Cheezie dust, pretzels, and beer caps.

Kimmy went outside to build sandcastles with the girls, leaving Mandy to clean up the mess.

NOW, ON THE FIRST visit with their father since he dropped them home at the end of the summer, cranky and sunburnt with sand in their shoes, his apartment felt empty and cool after the sultry buzz of those long hot days at the cottage. It was even worse with Mandy gone. The sound of her cries in the hallway the night before haunted Kimmy's thoughts, sending a chill deep into her belly.

Suddenly, she did not want to be there. She wanted to be home. And she wanted to tell her father that she could no longer visit him every weekend. She worried he would be angry. Or hurt. Or both.

When Fran asked about Mandy again, Phil suggested they go bowling. Stepping through the door of Frankie's Five-Pin Alley, Kimmy was swamped by the smell of feet and French fries, of beer, ammonia, and laminated wood. After trading in their runners for red and black shoes with shiny soles, she stood at the line cradling the mini pockmarked bowling ball, oily from the hands of hundreds, while Fran raced her palms over a steel globe immersed in a water bath.

Lola yelled at Fran to hurry up. Fran ignored her, so Lola threw a doll at her and hit Kimmy in the back of the head. Kimmy dropped her ball and ran after Lola, but her father grabbed her by the arm. Furious at being thwarted, Kimmy swung her fist and smacked him on the shoulder. He tossed her towards the seat and yelled at Fran who was still whipping her hands over the watery ball.

"Enough Fran. Sit down."

They finished the game in awkward silence, interrupted only by brief blips of chatter between Lola and Fran. As their father tallied the score, Kimmy's sisters ran off to the pinball machines. They hit the buttons on the side, banging the bumpers impotently because they had no money, and neither was willing to ask their dad.

Back at the apartment, their father retreated to his bedroom while Lola and Fran fought over the remote control for the TV. Kimmy walked out onto the concrete balcony off the living room. Clutching the top of the railing, its metal lip digging into her palms as she peered over, her fear of heights warred with a strong, stray urge to hurl herself up and over the barrier. Instead, she kicked at the thin vertical sheets of metal, the only thing between her and twenty floors of drop, a thunder-like reverberation echoing through the cool afternoon air.

The balcony door slid open and her father told her to come inside and set the table. As she pulled out the dinner plates, she saw a white ceramic smiley face mug shoved in the back of the shelf. A Father's Day gift from the year before. Did he save it or set it aside? The distinction between the two blurred.

Dinner was the divorced dad special – roast beef, baked potatoes and canned green beans.

"Leave some for the rest of us," Phil said after Kimmy took a large helping of meat.

"I want some too," said Fran as she grabbed at the plate, knocking her glass over, spilling water across the table.

"For Christ's sake, Fran. Clean that up. Now," said Phil, banging his hand against the dining room table, cutlery clanking against each other.

"Leave her alone," Kimmy said.

Her father raised his hand. She leaned forward as if defying him to hit her.

He let his arm drop, turned towards the kitchen, and hollered, "Fran, are you getting a towel?"

The next morning, he drove them back home to their mother. When he pulled into the driveway, it was devastatingly easy for Kimmy to tell her dad she wouldn't be visiting him next weekend. Because of school, she said. Probably not the next one either, she added. She was going to get a part-time job.

Standing on her front lawn, Kimmy raised her hand to wave goodbye. But her father had already turned away.

Blind Corners

THEY SAY YOU DON'T dream in a coma, but I dreamt of Beth.

In my dream, I was strolling down a dark foggy street and ran into an old friend from high school. She said Beth was alive, that it was all a mistake.

When I open my eyes, I'm lying in a hospital. My head is pounding, and the woman in the bed next to me is chattering about her inflamed gall bladder, her niece the driving instructor, and her poodle Petunia who keeps peeing on her sister's floor.

I'm in Auckland. And it wasn't a mistake.

Beth Wong, my first love and my first heartbreak, is gone.

"You're awake," says Annie, rushing into the room.

She sits on the bed beside me and puts a hand on my leg. Her fingernails, which she's bitten to the quick, lie jagged and bloody against the faded white sheet.

"Are you okay, Trish?"

I shake my head slowly, afraid of setting off another wave of throbbing.

"I'll get the doctor," she says, standing up quickly. Then, she's gone.

I stare at the dull white wall ahead of me as the sound of clattering trays in the hall and voices over the intercom clamour around me. The smell of food, warm and salty, wafts through the open door.

I close my eyes, trying to figure out how I ended up in this place. Scattered images swirl through my mind. Driving in the rain. An underground cave. Misty mountains and hot springs. A string of lights inside the darkness.

None of it makes sense.

Annie enters the room, bringing a woman with a stethoscope slung around her neck like a thin snake, and a gust of cool air. It stirs something in me, and I can't quite reach it. I tell the doctor my memories are a mess.

"That's to be expected," she says.

Annie peppers her with questions. Their voices meld, syllables crashing together. Words form and buzz around my head like a swarm of hornets: coma, accident, recovery, rest. I should pay attention, but my mind drifts. Then, the door closes and it's just me and Annie.

"When can I get out of here?" I ask.

"You heard the doctor. She wants to keep you overnight, to play it safe."

Why am I so eager to leave? Where would we go?

"How are you feeling?" Annie asks. She looks tired, bruised, her hair gone wild in the humidity.

"Shitty," I say. "What happened?"

"You don't remember?"

Annie, who loves the Go-Go's, magic realism, her Abyssinian cat, and me, squeezes my hand and tells me there was nothing that could have been done. When we drove around the corner, the vehicle coming towards us was already in a full-on skid. The teenage driver of the other car wasn't hurt, Annie banged up her knee and I ended up in a coma.

"Excuse me," the woman in the next bed calls. "Can you help me?"

Annie lets go of my hand. I lift my arm as if to stop her from leaving. She squeezes my leg, says she'll be right back, and passes over to the other side.

"Oh, hello, my dear," the woman says. "I've dropped my knitting. Can you get it for me?"

I sit up slowly. Through a gap in the curtain, I watch Annie pick up the wool. The woman grabs her wrist and says, "Is Jesus your personal saviour?"

"I, uh..."

"What lovely brown eyes you have. Just like my niece, Samantha. She's coming to see me today. Such a thoughtful child. Do you have an aunt, dear?"

"Yes, two. Back in Canada."

"And do you visit them? You know when I was your age, I went to Canada once. Lovely country. All those trees. Just lovely."

"Yes. I should get back to my friend."

"Is it serious?" the woman whispers. "I myself am quite ill. My doctor told me I'm lucky to be alive. First the gall bladder. Now they're saying there's something wrong with my liver. He's never seen one that big. Can't fix it. Can't take it out. They'll do what they can to ease my pain. Not that they've done such a great job of that. Still, if the good Lord can put his own son to suffer on a cross, I can cope with a touch of crippling pain."

"That's awful," says Annie. "But I should..."

"Yes, yes, of course. Could you ask one of the nurses to come see me. I'm really in a great deal of pain."

"I'll see if I can find someone," Annie says. She mouths to me that she'll be right back as she goes out into the hall.

I stare at the woman who sits upright in her bed, a ball of blue wool and needles in her lap. A wave of nausea washes over me. I lie back, close my eyes, and wait for it to subside.

I REMEMBER the flight here. It's one thing to know you'll be on a plane for fifteen hours and quite another to sit in a confined place through four meals and three movies while fighting the urge to fling open the emergency door. As the plane started its descent, my first glimpse of ocean surf and swaths of green hills made me forget all those cloistered hours in a hive of recycled air.

We stepped into a beautiful subtropical morning and caught a bus to the crowded, rickety youth hostel recommended by our Lonely Planet guidebook. The room consisted of two single beds, a wobbly wooden desk with an orange plastic lamp, and a peephole we discovered just before turning out the lights.

As Annie pulled duct tape out of her knapsack, I thought I saw an eye peering in. I ripped off a piece of tape, covered the hole, and ran the heel of my hand back and forth across it. We squished together into one of the single beds. Annie conked out immediately while I lay beside her, wide awake. Eventually I fell asleep, only to be startled awake in the middle of the night by angry yelling.

Annie rushed to the window and pushed aside the tattered curtains. I looked over her shoulder as a man stomped up the hill toward the hostel. When he reached the parking lot, he walked straight to the car we'd rented that afternoon from a lot down the road and swung something hard against it, the sound of metal-on-metal reverberating in the stillness. Then he wandered off into the night screaming a mélange of garbled words.

"We should do something," I said, meaning I wanted her to do something.

"Like what?"

"I don't know. Tell somebody?"

"Go ahead if you want. He's gone now. I'm going back to sleep," she said, climbing into her own bed.

I stood alone in the middle of the room, the moonlight through a gap in the curtains illuminating the strip of tape in the middle of the wall.

"Should we report the peephole?" Annie asked the next morning.

"Feel free," I said, still angry she hadn't done anything the night before.

I went down to check on the car. There was a dent in the frame above the taillight, which was miraculously still intact. The car was damaged, but still drivable — an inauspicious start to our journey. As if driving on the wrong side of the road wasn't challenging enough with the main highway changing moods more often than a hormonal teen. We'd be barrelling down a regular two-lane road one minute; the next, we'd be on a narrow country lane stopped cold by a herd of sheep meandering on their way to wherever sheep go.

ANNIE RETURNS, bringing a nurse for the old woman and another cold waft of air. This time, I remember being perched on a rubber tube, floating down a stream clad in a wetsuit and helmet. As Annie and I entered the cold, dark cave, we held on tight to the ropes connecting us so we wouldn't crash into the walls. The cavern smelled dank and fetid, its closeness stifling. A scattershot of white beams from our headlamps bouncing across the moist, craggy walls.

The guide told us to turn off our lights. Everything went black and still. Except the gleaming landscape above us. A mass of glowworms clustered on the ceiling, their spun silken threads hanging down to snare unsuspecting prey. We gazed up, enraptured by the flickering lights of a thousand pulsing creatures — a glowing sky inside a stone chamber deep beneath the earth's surface.

It reminded me of lying on my back beside Beth in the park as we stared up at the stars, our fingers intertwined, our breathing in synch. A moment trapped in time. Nothing else existed. No past, no future.

Beth and I were science geeks and long-distance runners who learned early on not to trust the ground beneath our feet. Growing up in Richmond, a boring suburb on the outskirts of Vancouver, the constant threat of the Big One hovered over our lives. We were told to stand in a doorway at the first sign of an earthquake, the way previous generations of schoolchildren were trained to duck-and-cover, assured by experts that a flimsy desk was the perfect shield against an atomic blast.

All through high school, Beth and I were obsessed with the idea of the earth rising against us.

"When do you think it will happen?" she asked one day as we lounged on the grass watching the Grade 9 gym class.

"Who knows? Maybe today."

She punched my arm. "Stop it. I mean really…"

"What? It could," I said as the field full of girls ran hurdles and hopped, stepped, and jumped into large damp sandpits.

Like children wanting, and not wanting, to be terrified by their daddy pretending to be a monster, we spent hours studying the cause and effect of the fierce upheavals that threatened to surge from beneath the earth. Then we'd run long and hard across its precarious surface.

I was going to get my PhD in geology and teach at UBC and Beth was going to travel the world studying plate tectonics and fissure vents.

"What do you think your parents will say?" I asked.

"I don't care. I'm doing it anyway."

"Me too," I said, still believing anything was possible.

EIGHT YEARS LATER, I spent my days extolling the virtues of hot springs and paint pots to a gaggle of tourists in Kootenay National Park, the career outcome of my barely achieved master's degree.

In the off-season, I rented a room in a house in Calgary with a rotating roster of artists, musicians, grad students, and anarchists. The house reeked of turpentine, treatises, and jam sessions. It made for a lively yet lonely existence for a girl and her rocks.

I met Annie when she joined one of my guided hikes. She was the only one who laughed at the shots of humour I slipped into my practiced patter about rock strata and magma chambers.

Lingering afterwards, she quizzed me on the migratory habits of ungulates, then asked me out for dinner.

A few months later, back in Calgary, we sat on the orange shag rug in my living room eating take-out curry and drinking Molson Canadian. My roommate Liz, an animal rights activist with three cats and a mangy old dog named Rex, joined us. I agreed with her and Annie that animals shouldn't be harmed, what else was there to say about it? Quite a lot apparently.

In the middle of Liz and Annie's impassioned discussion about puppy mills and cosmetics testing on bunnies, Annie reached over and nabbed one of my chunks of tandoori chicken.

"Hey," I said, putting my arms around my plate.

She laughed and started stabbing her fork in the direction of my food. I pushed her arm and scooted away. Startled, she blushed and stared down at the floor.

There was silence until Liz broke the tension by asking Annie if she'd ever considered becoming a veterinarian.

"Yes. But I couldn't get in."

"I didn't know that," I said.

"It's not exactly what you lead with when you're trying to impress a girl. It's kind of embarrassing."

"It shouldn't be. I've heard it's really hard to get into vet school."

"Yeah, let's go with that."

"At least you tried," I said. "I didn't even bother applying to the PhD program. I knew it was a lost cause."

"You still could," Annie said. "Me, I've already shot my load. Tried, failed, bought the t- shirt and moved on."

It was not a surprise then, how excited she was when she was offered the job as a vet's assistant in Vancouver. The next-best-thing to her dream job. She asked me to go with her. I was reluctant. Too much past in that place.

I suggested we go on a trip to celebrate before she started her new job. She wasn't much of a traveller, she said. All she wanted was a small house with a garden and chickens. I said New Zealand would be benign, easy. The perfect cautious first adventure for two young women who'd never travelled outside of North America.

I said nothing about dormant dreams of chasing earthquakes and volcanoes.

In the end, she let me talk her into flying halfway around the world, and I let her believe I'd move to the West Coast with her when we returned.

"DO YOU WANT me to call your parents?" Annie asks as she hands me a coffee from the hospital cafeteria.

"No."

"Don't you think they'd want to know?"

"I don't care."

"Trish."

"No."

Between my crappy job and disappointing girl-dates, I didn't need them to have one more reason to question my "life choices" as they put it. Getting in a car accident on my first overseas trip would only trigger their ever-ready "I told you so" reflex.

"Please," I said. "I'm fine. I'll call them later."

Annie looked at me as if I was struggling to learn a new language and wasn't saying what I thought I was saying.

"It's up to you," she said. "I'll call the airline this afternoon."

"Why?"

"To change our tickets. So we can go home."

"We don't need to do that."

"Of course we do. Did you think we were just going to carry on as if nothing happened?"

WHEN WE'D LEFT Auckland in our damaged car, we headed straight to Napier, the reason I'd wanted to come to New Zealand in the first place. The city was decimated by an earthquake in 1931. And, like Jesus rising from the dead, it resurrected itself as a monument to modernism when the entire downtown was rebuilt during an Art Deco blip in architectural history.

I pored over tourist brochures as Annie drove, I don't remember arriving or what we did when we got there. What I do remember is that sixty years after the city was wiped out, I stood in a red phone booth on an old-timey street rife with decorative sunbursts, hipped roofs, and stained glass, and called home. It felt like a small, cheerful miracle to hear my sister's voice, delayed and choppy over the distance. She caught me up on family doings, then said, "Oh, by the way..."

Surrounded by a riot of cotton candy-coloured buildings, far from home, I heard that Beth was dead. I hung up, pressed my forehead against the cool glass of the phone booth and tried to make sense of my sister's words.

BETH AND I had been best friends since Grade 8. Then, standing in a dark hallway at a party, both of us drunk and horny and sixteen, she leaned in and kissed me. And everything changed. When the lights came on, we sprang apart as if from a rug-induced shock. We ignored each other the rest of the night, then left at the same time. Without speaking, we walked deep into the park, away from streetlights and playgrounds. We kissed again and I thought my chest would burst open.

At our study date in the library the next day, I was afraid to look at her. Afraid that if I started, I would never be able to look away again. Beth nodded her head in time to the rhythm of her leg, which was bouncing up and down like a piston beneath the large wooden table. She could never sit still. That's why she ran. It was the only way to keep her jittery energy under control.

She gestured for me to come look at a book about the Pacific Ring of Fire, the region where 90% of the world's earthquakes occur. I sat beside her, conscious of our arms almost touching, of the pulse of desire in the space between us. Later, we went to the park. I stood with my back against a towering oak tree, its bark digging into my shoulders when I pulled her to me.

"DID YOU KNOW that another earthquake could wipe out this town all over again?" Annie asked when she returned from cruising Napier's souvenir shops.

"What?"

"All these beautiful Art Deco buildings could crumple like sandcastles. They're supposed to be earthquake proof but... And did you know that structures are less likely to get damaged if they're able to sway when the earth moves? Weird huh?"

"Fascinating," I mumbled.

"Are you okay?"

"I'm fine."

"Did you get through to your family?"

"No," I said, walking towards the car, clutching my grief greedily to my chest.

AS THREATENED, the old woman's niece has arrived at the hospital. She is crisp and efficient with short black hair. Opening her bag, she pulls out a tiny poodle and sets it on the ground, its nails clicking across the floor. The old woman squeals with delight as Petunia prances over to her and piddles on the floor beside her bed.

"Bad dog, Petunia," Samantha says, yanking paper towels from beside the sink and wiping up the mess. She tosses the towels into the garbage and scrubs her hands ferociously.

"I can't stay long," she says. "I have to get back to Mother."

"You just got here."

"She's not well. Her arthritis is so bad she can barely get out of bed."

"Oh, I know all about that. Sometimes my pain gets so bad, well, it's a good thing I get my comfort from the good Lord Jesus."

Samantha edges away from her aunt. She asks us where we're visiting from and if we've seen the Craters of the Moon.

"It's this fantastic geothermal field north of Taupo," she says.

"Yes," I say, remembering the smell of warm rotten eggs.

AFTER NAPIER we'd gone to the glowworm cave and from there we'd driven to a lodge near Rotorua where we soaked in a thermal pool and watched the dusky light sweep across the surrounding hills. A pair of girls ran squealing across the slippery deck as Annie reached for my hand beneath the churning water of the whirlpool.

Slipping from her grasp, I swam to the weird faux cave at the other end. Inside, it was gloomy and cool. Annie came in after me, but I ducked out the other side and went up to our room.

"What the hell?" she said when she found me lying in bed watching TV.

"I got chilled," I said.

"You could have told me you were leaving."

Still damp from the pool, she slid in beside me. I reached for her, but she turned away. I lay on my back and stared up at the nubs of plaster hanging from the ceiling.

The next morning, we drove to Taupo to see geysers in the wild. Ambling along wooden boardwalks, we watched for gusts of steam. We stopped at a spot that seemed more active than the others, a tangy sulphur smell lingering in the air as we waited for the roiling liquids that churned beneath the rocky surface to rip through the sky.

"Beth's dead," I said.

"Who? From high school?"

I nodded.

Annie put her hand on the fence separating us from the geyser field and asked me what happened. I shrugged. Hazy streams of mist leaked up through the rock, I'd grown weary of waiting for the geyser to strike.

"How did you find out?" she asked.

"I talked to my sister when we were in Napier."

Annie stared at me. "That was three days ago."

Back in the car, she asked me how I was. "Really," she said, touching my arm.

"I'm okay," I said, turning the radio knob, trying to find music between the clouds of static. "Maybe we should drive up to Whangarei."

Annie sighed and said, "Sure, if that's what you want."

THE FIRST TIME I lost Beth was in Grade 12. We only had one class together and she started hanging out with a new group of girls. I'd see them sitting together in the lunchroom. A self- contained unit. No room for anyone else. One day I went up and said hi to Beth. She was polite but distant, while the other girls looked at me suspiciously. When I walked away, I heard "Dyke" shout-whispered at my back.

The next morning when I opened my locker, I found my favourite green sweater, the one Beth wore nonstop the previous winter, on the shelf beside my geography textbook. When I pulled it out, a pair of black and white pictures fluttered to the floor.

We'd taken them at one of those old photo booths in the mall our first year of high school.

She sat in my lap and we made goofy fourteen-year-old faces at the camera. Afterward, Beth ripped the photo strip in half, giving me the lower two, and keeping the top ones for herself.

Crouching down, I picked up the pictures by the jagged bottom edge and tucked them into my back pocket. I carried them around for months, until the day I found them in my freshly washed jeans, reduced to a crumpled wet wad.

ANNIE SITS BESIDE me on my hospital bed, her shoulders hunched, her clothes stained and disheveled.

"I was so scared." Annie wipes her tears with the back of her hand. "That sound when your head hit the windshield...it was awful. You were in shock. You weren't making any sense. We flagged down another car and you passed out on the way here. I didn't know what to do."

I lie back on the pillow.

"Do you remember anything?" she asks.

"The early part of the trip is pretty clear, and some other bits and pieces of are starting to come back."

I rub my temples. Beneath the fog of medication, I can still feel a dull pulse of pain.

"I had a dream about Beth," I say.

"You never told me what happened to her?"

"According to my sister, the obituary said she died suddenly. It didn't give any details."

"Oh," Annie says.

"What?"

"My aunt told me that 'died suddenly' often means suicide."

"That's not what happened," I say, pulling my hand away from hers.

"Okay," Annie says, smoothing the sheet beside my legs.

I turn onto my side with my back toward her and curl up into a ball.

"Trish?" She places her hand on my hip.

I say nothing. Eventually, she moves away, and I feel the empty space where her hand had been.

"I'm going home as soon as I can change my ticket," she says.

I ignore her.

"Let me know if you want me to change yours too," she says.

Then, another whiff of cool air as she leaves the room.

I LOST CONTACT with Beth soon after moving to Calgary. At first, I phoned whenever I came home. She never called back. Once, I even went to her parents' door, and they said she wasn't in. I parked down the street, waited for her to come out and followed her to the mall. She cried when she saw me, then jumped in her car and drove away.

I let her go.

A couple of months later, I heard she was working for her father and engaged to the son of one of his business associates. My sister saw them together on the street one day. She said the fiancé seemed sweet, but Beth looked gaunt, unwell.

THE DOOR TO my room opens.

"I thought you were gone," I say, sitting up.

"I'm right here," Annie says, placing a coffee and a muffin on the table beside me. She pulls the chair away from my bed and sits down. Biting her fingernails, she taps her foot against the dreary hospital linoleum and stares at the curtain separating us from the woman next door.

We'd encountered a number of dodgy stretches of highway on our trip, it was nothing like what we saw on the Northland Peninsula. I remember driving through the rain toward Whangarei when the road turned to gravel. Then, it would periodically narrow to a single lane and disappear around a tall rock face. The last thing I recall was the angry slap of windshield wipers, the steep drop-off on our left, and the steering wheel beneath my hands as we rounded yet another blind corner.

I close my eyes and reach for Annie's hand.

Breakfast in Kenora

THE ENGINE LIGHT came on just outside Kenora.

Claire was on her way home to Toronto. She'd intended to drive straight through to Thunder Bay without stopping. Instead, two hours after leaving Winnipeg, she pulled into a garage on the edge of a small northern Ontario town. The mechanic said they were backed up, they would look at her car as soon as they could. She asked about a restaurant nearby. He pointed her to the Heart Hope Café down the street.

The rain was coming down hard, the wind blowing, the sky dark. She didn't have an umbrella, so she grabbed a plastic bag from her backseat, put it over her head and hurried through the downpour. She entered the restaurant, took a seat in the corner and watched the rain blowing against the glass.

Storms in August were the worst. Winter was supposed to be cold and ugly, but summer in Canada was too short for bad weather. It was like taking pennies from a homeless woman. Too cruel to be a mere crime.

The waitress placed a cup on the table in front of her. "Coffee?"

"That would be great. Thank you."

"Nasty out there, isn't it? Can I get you anything else?"

"Nothing for now, thanks."

"My name's Mina. Holler if you need anything."

The aroma of maple-tinged bacon wafted through the restaurant, tugging at a hunger Claire didn't know was there. She'd left her mother's house without eating, in a rush to get on the road. The bell over the door sounded and the smell of rain blew in, mingling with the odours of fried meat, butter, and a hint of bitter coffee.

The wind continued blowing outside as Claire sat with her arms on the slick Formica tabletop. She did not want to be there. She wanted to be crying alone in her car listening to Bonnie Raitt and eating chocolate-covered almonds by the handful. She should be deep into her journey home, letting distance unravel her knotty emotions instead of bristling in a public place, the clatter of cutlery and voices crashing through her thoughts.

The restaurant was busy for a blustery Tuesday morning. Claire watched Mina who was graceful yet awkward, like a fawn learning to walk on ice, never quite getting the rhythm right. She was chatty and charming with people who just wanted their eggs delivered warm, while she missed other tables completely.

One guy growled at her to bring his damn breakfast when she asked him if he needed more coffee. She smiled and poured the coffee then moved to another table. He yelled at her from across the room that she forgot his milk. She rushed back with a bowl of creamers while another woman tried to get her attention. The cook banged the bell. Then banged it again.

Her hunger enflamed by the greasy, rich smells of breakfast frying, Claire ordered an omelet and home fries. When Mina delivered the food, she lingered, asking her what brought her to Kenora, only to rush off in the middle of Claire's tale of vehicle woes, when a raised voice called out, "Excuse me, miss. This is not what I ordered."

Claire ate quickly, glancing periodically at her cell. No calls. The bell over the door sounded again and again, as people came and went while she stared at the glowing icons, willing her phone to ring.

WHEN HER SISTER Barb first invited her to come home to Winnipeg for a couple of weeks, Claire was wary. Her visits with family tended to last, at most, a couple of days. She became overwhelmed quickly. Too much talk. Too much people.

There was a reason she was a computer programmer. Machines

didn't feel the need to discuss things. They simply did what she told them to do. If her code was sloppy, the program spit out crap. If there was a flaw in her logic, the job would get caught in an endless spinning loop of nothingness. When she did it right, though, she mapped out cause and effect – if this, then that – in a perfectly orchestrated, vast complexity of triggers and events.

Programming was Claire's panacea for life's melted grape freezie emotions, that squishy purple mess she stepped into every time she visited family. The idea of spending more than a week with them felt daunting.

Their mother was getting on and her sister hinted at Alzheimer's. She said it might be the last time to see Mavis alert and coherent. Barb tended to toss out worst case scenarios like an artist flinging paint against a canvas to create a riot of colour.

Claire found her exhausting.

It was true. There was a shift in Claire's conversations with her mother. One time, in the middle of a chat about greenhouse tomatoes, Mavis went off on a diatribe about noisy garbage trucks, only to stop dead mid-sentence, place the phone down and wander away. Claire kept calling to her through the abandoned receiver until Mavis picked it up again, and resumed listing the ways in which tomatoes grown under glass were inferior to "normal" tomatoes.

A CRASH.

The room was startled into silence as Mina crouched beside a mess of broken plates, half- eaten pancakes, and a cluster of forks and knives that lay scattered across the floor. A mocking laugh came from the kitchen and the customers began to murmur, conversations picking up where they'd left off.

Claire walked towards the washroom. "You okay?" she asked as Mina dumped a tray full of shards into the garbage pail by the cash register.

"Yeah, thanks. Just another day at the races for this klutz."

When Claire came back to her table, her coffee cup was refilled.

She called the garage, they hadn't looked at her car yet. Breathing deeply, she sat up straight, holding her hands in her lap as she tried to stave off the jittery panic building inside.

"Can I get you anything else?" Mina asked.

"No, but thanks for the coffee."

"Any luck with the car?"

Claire shook her head.

"Just not our day, is it," Mina said.

Eventually, Barb wore Claire down and she agreed to make the trip home. The last time she'd driven to Winnipeg was years ago with Patti. It was Patti's first time travelling north of Lake Superior and she'd been shocked at the expanse of water that appeared before them when they came around a curve, not expecting to encounter a mini ocean in the middle of the Canadian Shield. Seeing the familiar landscape through Patti's eyes reminded Barb of its magnificence.

That thrill of rediscovery was missing this time around. There were only hours and hours of emptiness. Barren lands. Abandoned houses. Miles of forest and rock. The repetition, the endlessness, the steady hum of tires on asphalt, the brisk whoosh of a passing truck, and the bursts of cars speeding past, fleeing the place she was headed towards. Romantic in theory, tedious in reality, the drive was fatigue-flecked monotony interspersed with the odd glimpse of the spectacular. Much like her love life.

Claire pulled into the parking lot of Old Woman Bay and walked through the shaded tree cathedral leading to the sandy beach where she and Patti had ambled contentedly all those years ago. Before things imploded. Before she started seeking the soft landing of another.

Like a bodyguard scanning a rooftop for an assassin's gun, Claire searched for a new love whenever the current one came under threat. Moving on easily, as if blithely stepping from one boulder to the next, her feet never touching the ground.

After her most recent girlfriend left, perhaps sensing that shift in Claire's attention, she didn't have the heart to try again. Two years later, alone on a desolate shore, she realized it had been ten years since she'd stood there with Patti, the one she'd never wanted to lose.

She stared out at the finger spits of beach poking out into the water, the sand along the edges darkened by the wash of waves. An arboreal graveyard with stripped, empty branches sprouting from the ground. Random brush, rotting logs, and tiny tendrils of dried tree trash scattered across the heavily trodden sand.

The drive was supposed to help ease the transition from her quiet life to the emotional minefield of family. She didn't anticipate was how tiring it would be. By the time she arrived in Winnipeg she felt spent, her nerves exposed and raw. After the steady bruising drip of Trans-Canada Highway tedium, the sudden plunge into Barb's swirling fuss was disorienting.

As soon as she entered the house, her sister asked, "What are we going to do about Mom?" As if barbarians were at the gate and they were fresh out of boiling oil to pour from the turrets.

"What do you mean, what are we going to do about her?" Claire asked tossing her keys onto the counter.

"She's losing it."

"Can I maybe get a drink? Or five or six?"

"Reg, grab Claire some wine. The one in the fridge door. White okay?"

"Yeah, sure, anything. Hey, Reg."

"Hi Claire. Welcome to Winnipeg," he said handing her a glass of Chardonnay.

She sat on the couch and took a large gulp.

"How was the drive?" Barb asked.

"Long." Claire took another swig. The wine tasted cool and acidic.

"Do you want anything to eat?" her sister asked.

"No, thanks. Where's Mom?"

"I told her it would be best if she stayed home tonight, that you'd be tired after your trip."

"Why didn't I go straight to her place then?"

"We need to talk," said Barb.

Claire sat back wearily. Trying to divert her sister when she was on a mission was like throwing balls of fire into the ocean to take off the chill. A futile effort and a waste of perfectly good fireballs.

"I don't know how much longer she can keep living on her own.

When her washing machine stopped working, do you know what she did?" asked Barb incredulously, shaking her head. "She stopped doing her laundry. Can you believe that? She didn't tell us her machine was broken. She just went around in her stained, wrinkled clothes until we figured out what was happening. Thank God for Reg. He fixed the washer and got her back on track. I'm not sure how I'd cope without him. It's not like she'll listen to me."

Barb bent forward, her arms resting on her thighs. "It can't go on like this. What are we going to do?"

Claire turned away from her sister's intensity. After two straight days of driving, her mind was sludge. She could barely register the cacophony of cars honking outside, or the stuttering on and off of water rushing into the kitchen sink, as Reg did the dishes. And she certainly wasn't up to combating Barb, who wielded her emotions like a blunt weapon.

"What can we do?" Claire asked, sighing. "It's not like we can force her to wash her clothes."

Wrong answer.

"IS EVERYTHING OKAY?"

Claire looked up.

"You were shaking your head," Mina said.

"Sorry, yes, all good."

Claire noticed that the restaurant was empty. Outside, the storm intensified. Huge drops of water blew into the window like handfuls of pebbles flung by a love-soaked teenager enticing her crush to come out in the rain.

"So where were you off to before you got stranded here?" Mina asked.

"Toronto."

"Is that home?"

"I guess. I live there. I grew up in Winnipeg so that's also kind of home. Though not really anymore."

"Yeah, the 'Peg' is a good place to leave."

"You from there?"

"No," Mina said, sitting down at the table across the aisle from Claire's. "I lived there with my aunt for a couple of years in high school. That was good. Going back there for university was not. Flamed out my first year. The only good thing was this glassblowing course I took during spring break. You ever done it?"

"I tried pottery once and ended up with a jumbled mess of clay that looked like that Salvador Dali melting clock," said Claire. "So, no, it would not be a good idea for me to mess around with hot glass. What's it like?"

"Amazing. And weird. You blow through this long pole to form a bubble, like the shiny soap bubbles kids make with those wand thingies. And they're beautiful. Magical even. And so fragile."

The cook bustled out of the kitchen saying, "I gotta run out and pick up the kids. Can you hold down the fort? Won't be more than half an hour."

"Yeah, sure," Mina replied.

"Hubby was supposed to do it, but 'something came up'," the cook said, making sarcastic air quotes. "So, I gotta leave work so he can, I dunno, help his buddy fix his outboard motor or some other screaming emergency that prevents him from picking up his own damn kids from the neighbours. Where they had to go in the first place, mind you, because he was too busy to take care of them. I'm telling you, Mina, don't get married. You hear me? Worst mistake of my life. Back soon."

After the cook left, a quiet settled over the deserted restaurant. Claire gazed out the storm-soaked window until a wet bedraggled man knocked on the glass door of the café and peered in from the cramped entryway.

"Got anything to eat?" he asked.

Mina jumped up and went into the kitchen, emerging a few minutes later with a sandwich, which she held up towards him saying, "Plain old peanut butter. Just the way you like it."

She turned towards Claire and said, "Billy doesn't care for jam."

The man snatched the sandwich from her hand and fled, as if afraid she would take it back if he dared to linger. Claire watched Billy disappear into an alley across the road.

"So, how long were you in Winnipeg?" Mina asked.

"Since Sunday."

"You drove all the way there for a couple of days?"

"Well, it wasn't supposed to be that short a visit. It just turned out that way, what with me sneaking out of my mother's house in the dead of night and all," Claire said, looking down at the floor.

BY THE TIME Claire extricated herself from Barb's litany of frustrations and drove the three blocks to her mother's house, she was drunk with exhaustion, a barrage of her sister's complaints still pounding inside her brain. She pulled into the driveway and turned off the ignition. Dropping her forehead onto the steering wheel, she wondered why she'd come. Nothing good could possibly come of it.

They had a history, she and her sister.

When she was eight years old, Barb talked Claire out of her most prized possession, a battered hardcover version of *Harriet the Spy*, its pages smeared and torn by the relentless attentions of dirty hands, one corner of its cover dented from falling to the floor each night after Claire had fallen asleep reading it. Again.

Barb had been invited to a birthday party but didn't have time to get a present. The girl's name was Harriet, she'd said, and wouldn't it be great if she could have a book written about her? Claire reluctantly gave up this precious object, only to discover later that the birthday girl's name was Frances and her sister kept the book for herself.

"If you were willing to give it away to someone you didn't even know," Barb asked when confronted, "shouldn't you be willing to let your very own sister have it?"

Claire was ashamed to have fallen for Barb's transparent manipulation. A shame that flared up like a flashback reaction to past poisons, whenever she and her sister got together.

Claire stepped out of her car and noticed that the door of her mother's house was wide open. She grabbed her bag from the trunk and walked up the steps. It was late and she didn't want to startle her mom. She poked her head through the doorway and saw Mavis sitting in a chair in front of the TV, hands in her lap, staring ahead as if there was some riveting action on the blank screen in front of her.

"Mom, why's your door open?"

Her mother turned slowly towards her and, said, "I'm waiting."

"I haven't forgotten how to knock. You didn't need to leave it wide open."

"Did I?"

Claire dropped her bag in the hallway and stooped down to hug her mother, who smelled of dust and sweat.

"You okay?" Claire asked.

"Oh, yes, I'm very well, thank you. How are you?"

"I'm good. Long drive, but I'm happy to be here."

"We used to go for drives. The whole family. Every Sunday afternoon. Sometimes out to the Delta Marsh to watch the ducks, sometimes to Beaudry Park."

"Yes, I remember. The drive here was gorgeous, but it's a long trip from Toronto..."

"Oh," said Mavis, brushing her fingertips across her forehead, as if to clear a branch that was obscuring the view. "It's you."

"Who did you think it was?"

Mavis fluttered her hand in front of her face as if to wave away an unpleasant odour.

"Mom?"

Mavis stared at the floor and shook her head. Then, as if sloughing off a role she was playing on stage, she straightened her back, lifted her head and looked directly at Claire.

"Are you tired? I've made your bed and there's a towel if you want to have a shower. I always needed to get cleaned up after a long trip. Couldn't sleep until I'd washed the road off me."

"No, I'm fine. I think I'll go straight to bed," said Claire standing up. "Are you sure you're okay?"

"Now, don't you start. I get quite enough of that from your sister, thank you very much."

"Alright, we'll catch up in the morning. Good night."

Claire was anxious to quit the room but reluctant to leave her mother alone. She climbed the stairs, fighting the urge to check on her again, to call out one last time.

She fell asleep instantly and slept through the night. When she got up, there was a pot of coffee on the counter and porridge on the stove. The radio was playing softly, a morning talk show about disappearing wildlife habitat murmuring in the background, as her mother swept the floor. A normalcy postcard to fend off the skewed image from last night.

After breakfast, Claire suggested they go to a nearby spa for mother-daughter mani-pedis and a massage.

"Oh, what a wonderful idea," Mavis said. "Can I pick my own nail polish?"

"Of course you can."

When they arrived at Barb and Reg's, Mavis flashed her ruby nails proudly.

"Aren't you a little old for red?" asked Barb.

"Why can't you ever say anything nice? I think they're perfect. Thank you, Claire."

Barb raised her eyebrows as Mavis hugged Claire.

In the middle of lunch - mini quiches and crudités - Mavis stood up, walked to the porch door and called out to Freddie, their long-dead childhood dog. Claire avoided Barb's gaze as she put her hand on her mother's shoulder and led her back to the table. Mavis faltered, as if struggling to solidify the wavering landscape in her mind.

"I want something sweet," Mavis said. "Why is there never any dessert here?"

"Reg, why don't you take Mom out to see the garden while Claire and I clean up."

"I don't want to see the garden. I want cake."

"Reg?" Barb said, nodding her head towards her mother.

"Come on, Mavis, I've got some cookies in the cupboard. Then I'll show you our new marigolds."

Mavis stood up and followed Reg. Then she stopped and turned back to her daughters.

"What about Claire?"

"She's staying with me. We're going to chat."

"What about?"

"Sister stuff. You go on with Reg."

Mavis hesitated. She started to move towards her daughters. Then Reg touched her on the arm, and she let him steer her towards the backyard.

"She won't do anything I tell her to do but as soon as Reg asks, she's all, 'Yes, Reg, whatever you want, Reg'. It's the only way I'm getting through this. How was she last night?"

"A little confused..."

"I told you."

"But she's getting older. That's to be expected."

"Did she know who you were?"

"Yes, she knew who I was." Claire said, walking into the kitchen. She stood at the sink topping up her water glass and watched her mother and Reg strolling through the garden.

"Well, good for you," said Barb. "She sure the hell doesn't always know who I am. Though she always manages to remember to treat me like crap."

When she went back into the dining room, Claire found Barb with her hands in her lap staring at the old lace tablecloth, an inheritance from their grandmother who died in her sleep at age 92. A massive stroke, fast and fatal.

"Come on, it can't be that bad."

"Is that right? It's all very well for you to swoop in waving your credit card and whisk her away for a trip to the spa. You're not the one who has to nag her to take her pills every day."

"So don't."

"Really Claire? That's your solution?"

"I meant there's got to be another way."

Barb pursed her lips and glared at the wall above Claire's head.

"I'm sure it's hard though," said Claire, swallowing down a tangled skein of anger and shame.

"Damn right it's hard. I'm at my wit's end. You're like the divorced dad who swoops in to take the kids on a whirlwind trip to Disneyworld, then drops them home to Mom to deal with the sugar crash and tantrums. It's me who will have to cope with Mom if she falls or can't manage on her own anymore."

"What do you want me to do?" Claire asked.

"You don't get it do you?"

Claire looked at her sister who was staring at her, waiting. Claire shook her head. No, she did not get it. There was no tweak to the code she could make that would fix this. What was she supposed to do? What was she supposed to say?

"Why do I always have to be the bad guy? I can't...I'm done," Barb blurted, and stomped out.

Claire's stomach lurched, a wave of nausea shooting through her.

"Barb told me we have to leave," Mavis said, as she and Reg entered the room.

"You don't have to go. Barb thought you might want to take a nap or something. It's been a busy day..." said Reg, his voice trailing off.

"Yes," said Claire, her heartbeat stuttering like an engine with water in the line, "that's a good idea".

Driving back to Mavis's house, she wished she was alone, speeding past a blur of rocks and trees, on her way to someplace far from here.

When her mother lay down for a nap, Claire got back into her car and drove to Assiniboine Park. Strolling through the conservatory, she hoped the humid whiff of rose petals under glass would still her churning insides. Instead, her whole body throbbed like a festering wound in the tropics as she walked along the perfect rows of perfect flowers beneath the perfect sun.

Her mother was still asleep when Claire got home so she wandered through the house, looking for something to do, for a way to be useful. In the pantry, she found a shelf drooping under the weight of bags of flour and sugar and jars of almonds and raisins. She peeked underneath and saw the screws in the metal bracket jutting out from the wall, their bared ridges coated in white drywall dust. She pulled everything off the shelf and took it down. The screws were too short. She searched for something to replace them in her mother's junk drawer. All she found were a couple of steel spiral nails. Not ideal but at least they were longer than the screws.

She moved along the pantry wall tapping. When she heard the dull muffled sound of a stud, she used the tip of the nail to draw a small x in the wall then moved further down to find the next one. She lodged the board against the wall using the weight of her body and tried to hammer the hanging bracket quietly. It felt awkward and unwieldy but somehow, she managed to rig the shelf up. It seemed solid when she pushed down on it, so she loaded it up again and stood back, examining her work.

The whole thing collapsed so fast, she didn't have time to react. She reached her hand out just as a jar of coconut fell to the floor, scattering glass and toasted white flakes everywhere. Then, a cascade of falling walnuts, dried mangoes, basmati rice, and sugar, and a puff of bleached flour dust rising into the air, as jar after jar tumbled onto the pantry floor.

In the silence after the last jar broke, Claire heard the quiet rumbling snores of her mother who slept through the crash and shatter of her daughter's failed repairs. Claire grabbed the broom and dustpan. Staring down at the mess she'd made, she could not bear to tackle the cleanup. She left the pantry, closing the door behind her and returned to the living room to stare out the window at the shimmering heat rising from the road in front of her mother's house.

When Mavis woke from her nap, they prepared dinner together. A simple spaghetti and meat sauce with pre-packaged grated parmesan cheese from a green plastic container Claire remembered from childhood. She suspected it might be the very same one. Which didn't stop her from pouring liberal amounts of the chalky powder over her noodles.

She cleaned the kitchen while her mother drank a cup of mint tea at the table. Afterwards, they played a round of kitchen bridge, a game Mavis thought she remembered how to play but didn't. Claire went along with her mother's fluctuating rules, unable to muster the energy to care about shifting trump and unearned tricks.

Until Mavis accused her of cheating.

In a fit of pique, Claire threw her cards down on the table and stomped off to her room, like the ghost of her teenage self. Shame followed fast in anger's slipstream. She hid in her room the rest of the evening, waiting until her mother was asleep, then returned to the pantry to sweep up the glass shards mingled with nuts and chocolate chips.

She dumped everything into the garbage, propped the faulty shelf up against the back wall of the closet, shut the door, and went back to bed where she lay in the dark, bristling. Unable to sleep, she got up at 5 AM, packed her bag and left a note for her mother saying sorry, she'd been called back into work. She snuck out into the night, the only sound on the empty streets the soft metallic hum of streetlights.

At work, when she ran into trouble, when a computer program didn't work, Claire dug in, worked longer, harder, to make it right. With family, her first instinct was to give up. To take the fast fall rather than struggle to stay aloft on a wire that wavered and wobbled no matter what she did.

Claire gave Mina the abbreviated, less damning version of her fight and flight.

"Family's hard," said Mina.

"Yeah. My best relationship is with my dad and he's been dead ten years. Though even with him...I can still see him shaking his head at me in disappointment."

"Don't get me started on dads," Mina said as she walked to the coffee machine and held up the carafe towards Claire, who shook her head.

"My dad's still alive," Mina said. "He's so busy with his new wife and kids in Thunder Bay, I hardly ever see him. He'll probably have moved on to his third family before I get my first. Especially since the boys around here are looking for a wife they don't have to marry. They want all the frills and none of the work. Not that I wouldn't mind a guy willing to pick wild rice for me or talk me down from a reckless move, without expecting me to watch him play hockey Friday nights. The truth is, what I really want is a live-action Siri. Someone I can order around without having to make him feel good about himself."

Mina's phone rang. She picked it up and wandered towards the kitchen, saying, "No, Mom, I didn't ask Rachel to cover my shift..."

"Everything ok?" Claire asked when Mina sat back down.

"Oh, sure. You got any sisters or brothers?"

"A sister. You?"

"Yeah, I got one of those. I also have a brother who's this amazing sculptor. He has people falling all over themselves to rub up against his talent. Nothing rich people love more than buying themselves an artist. Sadly, there's no patron spewing out cash for this glassblowing, plate-smashing, dropout waitress. My mama, the band chief, is so proud," she said laughing.

"She'd had such big plans for me. I was going to become the first Indigenous Prime Minister. So close," Mina said, spreading her arms out in a Vanna White ta-da gesture towards the grease-streaked walls of the café, as if showing off her new desk in Parliament Hill.

"Good thing my sister's picking up the slack. She's this superstar good-deed activist lawyer awash in gold medals. In a couple of days, she's getting another award at the human rights museum."

"In Winnipeg?"

Mina nodded.

"Are you going?"

"I don't exactly work in an industry where they give you time off for award shows. Not that my mother understands that. She expects me to get the single mom with three kids to swap shifts so I can be there. Does she have any idea how much of a pain that would be for Rachel? And she would do it too. Which is why there's no way I'm asking her. Are you and your sister close?"

"We have our challenges," Claire said tapping on the surface of her silent phone as if responding to a nonexistent text. "So, are you still doing the glassblowing?"

"Unfortunately, there's no place to do it around here but I have started making these other cool things. Hold on, I'll show you."

Mina jumped up and went into the kitchen, returning with a greenish blue tadpole cupped inside her hand.

"It's called a Prince Rupert's Drop. You heat up a glass rod with a blow torch until it forms a drop, which you let fall into a glass of cold water. And you get this," she said handing it over to Claire.

"They're also called Dutch tears, and they're completely unbreakable. Well, part of them is unbreakable. You could take a hammer to this bit here," Mina said, tapping the bulbous body. "And nothing would happen. But if you damage this," she said pointing to the fragile looking filament of glass extending from the body, "the whole thing explodes. They have these videos on YouTube – you should watch them – they clip the tail and you can see the fracture spread in slow motion like a crashing wave. Then the whole thing shatters. Can you believe it? How it can go from liquid to solid then burst into glass dust, just like that?"

"Interesting," said Claire, handing the drop back just as her phone rang. It was the garage.

"Finally," she said as she hung up.

"It's ready?"

"Yup. I can get the hell out of here. Sorry, I didn't mean it like that."

"That's okay, I understand. You want to get home. So, listen, I want to thank you."

Claire looked up, furrowing her brow.

"I was having a shit day, and no one else bothered to even try to be decent. So, I'd like to give you something. For being kind to me."

She held out the Prince Rupert's drop.

Claire glanced away, embarrassed. "I can't accept that."

"Why not?"

Claire shrugged and looked at the ground. She wasn't kind, she was careless with her attention, good at feigning interest in others to disguise the churn of her own anxiety.

"Too much?" Mina asked. "I never get it right. Did you know I've been accused of being pathologically generous? Not by my family, of course. Apparently, I'm only nice to strangers. Though I did try to give my mom one of these. She was not impressed."

Mina gazed down at the Prince Rupert's drop in her outstretched hand.

"Can I buy it from you?" asked Claire, pulling some bills from her wallet. "It's really beautiful. And so unique."

She held the cash out to Mina who looked away. Claire set the money on the table quickly, eager to be rid of it.

"I love it." Claire took the Prince Rupert's drop. "Thank you."

They stood together in silence, both looking down at the shimmering globular glass in Claire's hand.

"Well, I should go pick up my car," she said, closing her fist over Mina's drop and grabbing her phone from the table.

"Yeah, sure," Mina said, moving towards the door. "So, what was wrong with it?"

"It seems the engine light came on because I didn't close the gas tank cap properly. Turns out my car's better than me at identifying problems. It's also no better than I am at diagnosing the cause."

Claire thanked Mina. For everything, she said, as she walked out of the restaurant.

The storm passed, though the sky remained dreary, the air dank and heavy. The streets were empty and black from the rain, a faint glimmer of sun peeking out from beyond faded dark clouds.

She pulled out from the garage parking lot and drove towards the highway. As she approached the crossroads, she didn't know which way she should go. Left, to return to Winnipeg, or right, to head home to Toronto.

Claire took a deep breath and pushed the turn signal down.

Patsy's Kitchen

THE FIRST TIME I saw Patsy was a week after she moved into the small clapboard house next door. I was in the attic poking around in boxes of papers and books looking for anything that wasn't dead boring, when I heard a clanging outside.

Peering out the dormer window, I saw a woman with red hair yanking a tattered yellow lawn chair out of the way as she pushed a clothes hamper with her foot towards a clothesline strung across her overgrown lawn. Her skinny arms shook out the sodden lumps of clothes and hung them on the line using the clothespins lodged between her pursed lips.

Then, shielding her eyes with her hand, she turned towards our house as if sensing my presence. I quickly stepped into the shadows and the hand she'd raised stopped in mid-air, as if she had started to wave at a loved one only to realise it wasn't them after all.

The next morning I hung around our back yard, sneaking looks between the slats of the tall wooden fence that ran along the edge of our property. I saw no sign of anyone next door and became distracted by an ant lugging a grain of rice twice its size towards a mound of sand with a tiny hole on top. I didn't notice that anyone was near until a voice spoke behind my left ear.

"What ya got there, kiddo?"

I looked up. The woman I'd watched the day before peered at me as I crouched over the ant like a dog hunched over its food dish waiting for something tasty to appear.

"Nothing," I said. "Just a dumb old ant."

"Well," she said, "if you're not currently tied up with any earth-shattering activity, perhaps you'd care to join me for some lemonade and chocolate chip cookies."

"Okay," I said hesitatingly.

"I'm Patsy," she said. "And what might your name be?"

"Sandy."

"Sandy," she said in a wistful tone, as if it was a name she'd never heard before, but that she liked and wanted to be sure not to forget. "Well come on over. I'll give you the fifty-cent tour of the place."

We walked onto the deck and through the back door into her house. On the right was an open door from which I could smell the dark moist stench of the cellar. Patsy pointed me towards the kitchen table where a mound of homemade cookies sat on a big blue plate. She grabbed a pitcher of lemonade from the fridge and poured me a glass, then filled the kettle and put it on top of the stove. She measured a teaspoon of instant coffee into a chipped white cup and lit a cigarette. Sitting down across from me, she blew smoke into the air above my face, then looked me straight in the eye.

"So, you on your own?"

"Yeah."

She nodded her head like she'd figured as much and said, "You and me both."

It was the first summer I was allowed to stay home alone while everyone else went to work. Usually I had to go to day camp where we made droopy clay ashtrays, ugly beaded belts, and other useless stuff that nobody would ever wear or use. I thought it would be great to have the house to myself, but instead the days were long and dull.

The kettle boiled and Patsy jumped up to make her coffee. While she did, I looked around the long narrow room with orange and brown patterned linoleum curled up slightly in the corner. Everything was neat and clean, and faded, like a shirt washed too many times.

Patsy returned to the table with her steaming cup and began to talk. The room was cool, a soft breeze blowing through the window. I sat back in my chair and listened as I munched cookies and drank glass after glass of sweet lemonade.

She'd grown up on a farm a couple of hours away, she told me. Her brother was twelve years older than her and was married and started up his own farm just down the road when she was only eight years old. Her nieces and nephews, a total of six of them when all was said and done, were more like sisters and brothers. She spent a lot of time over there babysitting and helping out Frank's wife Sissy, a gnarly runt of a woman who churned out the kids and could barely keep up with it all.

"It's not that she didn't try, course she did, but she just didn't have the strength to take care of all them kids plus run the household and help out with the haying in the fall. I don't know what they'd have done without me. Course, once the kids grew up, they were all able to help out and Sissy could just stay and work in the house. That poor woman was old before her time, right worn out with all that farming and drudgery. I think back now and she was only in her twenties but to me she was ancient, like a dried up husk of corn. She died young that one did. No surprise there. She got all her kids married off and out of the house. Then one morning she didn't get out of bed and the next day she was gone."

Patsy looked out the window as if seeing it all played out against the side of our house next door, her cigarette poised in front of her lips, its long ash curved perilously downwards. I watched intently, waiting for it to fall, and before it could, she swung her hand away from her mouth, stubbed out the cigarette and reached for another. Tiny wisps of smoke leaked upwards from the ashtray and a new full cloud appeared in front of her face.

When I went home, I felt sick and bloated from the sugar and the talk. Our house felt so quiet, so empty. A few minutes later my older sister Catherine came home from her lifeguarding job. She ran upstairs, banged drawers and ran water in the bathroom sink. I followed her and found her in her bra and panties, a towel wrapped around her head staring into the mirror. She fluttered her eyelashes as she held a stick loaded with thick black gunk close to her eyes. I stood in the doorway and watched.

"Do you mind?" she asked, shutting the door in my face.

I went back downstairs and sat out on the front steps in front of our place watching a handful of boys play street hockey and the Kramer twins hopscotching across the road. My mother came home from work lugging bags of groceries and her briefcase, and said, "I'll need you to set the table, Sandra, so don't wander too far away."

My father's car turned into the driveway. He walked across the lawn to where I sat, ruffled my hair, said, "How's my pumpkin today?" and entered the house.

The next day I gathered up my courage and knocked on Patsy's door.

"Hi, come on in," she said as if it was the most natural thing in the world for me to appear at her door. "I was just going to make myself a cup of coffee."

For weeks I appeared at her door every single day. I'd sit for hours on end, the backs of my legs stuck to the vinyl chair seat, across from Patsy and her endless stream of words and smoke.

With her I no longer felt like an astronaut lurching around on the moon, out of synch with the world on which I'd landed. I'd watch as she shoved the burning butt of her cigarette against the clean end of another, small orange strands wound tightly inside delicate white paper, and feel for once that I wasn't an unwanted visitor in my own life.

Until we made the mistake of venturing outside her kitchen. The image I'd created of someone who existed to make me feel cared for, listened to, wavered when exposed to the air beyond the confines of her wood-panelled walls and linoleum floors.

It was a late August morning when I told Patsy I had to stay in the night before because I hadn't cleaned my room well enough for my mother. "She's so picky..." I complained.

"Lord, don't I know picky," she interrupted. "I once had to rip out all the stitching I done on this apron for Mrs. Holmes in grade eight, just cause it wasn't as straight as a Baptist in church on Sunday..."

'Yeah, but my mom is mean," I whined.

"The best thing about Mrs. Holmes," Patsy continued as if I hadn't said a word, "was she let us play Bingo once a month. I sure did love that game. Haven't played it in ages. Hey, what do you say you and me go down to the Bingo Hall one of these days? We'll have us a girls' night out."

She looked at me all open and excited.

"I can ask," I mumbled.

That night I broached the subject at dinner. "Can I go to the Bingo Palace tomorrow night?"

My mother looked at me like I'd just asked her if I could move my bedroom out into the street and change my name to Pavement.

"Why on earth would you want to do that?" she asked dumbfounded.

"To play bingo maybe," I said in my, isn't-it-obvious, voice.

She looked at my father, then said, "I don't want you going there alone. You're too young."

"I wouldn't," I said. "I'd be there with an adult."

"Who?" she asked.

"Patsy."

"Who?"

"Patsy, our next-door neighbour."

She sat back in her chair and stared at my father.

"How do you know this Patsy?" he asked.

"She lives next door."

"Yes, I know she lives next door. Have you been spending much time with her?"

I shrugged. "I dunno, a bit."

"Why haven't you mentioned it?"

"What's the big deal?"

"There's no need to get snarky young lady."

"So, can I go or not?" I asked.

My father looked at my mother, then said, "Yes, just this once." He continued to eat his dinner ignoring the furious look my mother gave him.

I'd seen the dark hooded looks directed next door and heard the whispers about a dead child and a husband who did not stay. Which only made Patsy more appealing. Because I knew my parents also grumbled about me. I was bright, my report cards said, but didn't apply myself. The words bad and attitude were thrown together with frightening regularity. I was the gritty piece of sand in the precision machinery of a family that otherwise reeked of achievement.

Once again, I retreated to the haven of Patsy's kitchen where I felt safe from the judgements of others. When I told her I was allowed to go to Bingo, she looked pleased, which in turn pleased me. I showed up early to her place the next night. She had lipstick on, which I'd never seen her wear before. She looked even more nervous than usual, plucking non-existent lint from her pressed dress slacks and tugging at the collar of her blouse. Then, she drew her shoulders back and let her arms fall to her sides.

"Right," she said. "Off we go."

She walked quickly, leaving a tangy sweet puff of perfume in her wake, as I ran to keep up with her. As we entered the large parking lot in front of the Bingo Palace, clusters of women squeezing through the front door, she faltered, as if doubting her decision to leave the safety of her kitchen. Then, she forged ahead determinedly.

I stuck close to her as we joined the milling crowd. I sensed the other women avoiding her, averting their eyes whenever she smiled in their direction. She put her hand on my shoulder. For the first time, I felt the weight edge out the comfort.

We entered the large room filled with tables and chairs and a steady flow of chatter. She found us a spot at a table where a couple of women tapped the ends of their cigarettes into a silver ashtray already brimming with lipstick-stained butts. Succumbing to the intoxication of possibility, I greedily took the cards Patsy gave me. I lined them up in front of me and grabbed a handful of small red chips from the box in the centre of the table. The chips were cool and smooth and light. I let them sift through my partially closed fist onto the table in front of me, forming a small hill of flat plastic Smarties.

Patsy hunched over her cards, her eyes squinting with concentration as she scanned the lines of cards in front of her. Her hands, which normally fluttered and trembled, were strong and sure as she placed the markers down. When a woman across the room called Bingo, she let out a deep sigh and her shoulders slumped. She stood up and said she was going to the little girls' room.

"They say she was off gossiping at a neighbour's when that poor little boy got hit by a car," one of the women at the end of our table said.

"I heard she was passed out on home-made wine, in the middle of the afternoon no less," replied the other.

"Some people shouldn't be allowed to have children if you ask me. No wonder her husband left. Can't say I blame him."

The women clucked their tongues and shook their heads, as if there was no such thing as a random stroke of bad luck. I felt myself flush when their attention turned towards me, their voices lowering into guilty whispers. When Patsy returned, I couldn't look at her.

The cracks between us had already begun to appear and that night at the Bingo Hall only made them more obvious. I relished her attention because my family barely noticed me. I'd started to think that she might not be so different from them. That maybe she wasn't really interested in what I had to say. That I was simply the only audience available to her.

Neither of us won anything that night. After the last Bingo was called and we were leaving the building, I looked back at the women in blue smocks collecting the cards from amongst the refuse of discarded coffee cups and overflowing ashtrays.

When Patsy asked me if I'd enjoyed myself, I shrugged, looked away, and said, "It was okay," in a tone of voice that suggested it wasn't even that. When she invited me into her house for cookies and lemonade, for the first time ever, I refused.

I did not even have the decency to look at her.

I was so focused on my own victimhood that I chose to disregard all the past kindnesses she'd shown me. Willfully forgetting how I felt less lonely when I was with her. And how I, for once in my life, was capable of making someone else feel less lonely.

Instead, I punished her for not being who I needed her to be. I was smart, and for once, I applied myself. Learning to treat her the way others did, doing to her what others did to me. As if that might somehow fix everything.

The next day I hid in the attic and watched her in her yard as she pulled out dandelions.

She glanced over at our house several times, I stayed well out of sight. Finally, she went inside, sadly, serenely, as if she was sorry, but not surprised, to be left alone yet again.

A Tidy Woman

FROM A DISTANCE, the waterfall appeared to plummet straight into the earth. Margaret walked to the edge of the cliff and looked down to see the water streaming into a hidden crevice before rushing downstream in a flurry of white waves.

A strong breeze blew across the canyon. She stepped back and swept her hand across her brow, trying, and failing, to keep her hair out of her face. Giving up, she hung her head, closed her eyes and let the wind have its way.

"Incredible, isn't it?"

Margaret looked up to see a woman coming towards her.

"Most spectacular place on earth," the woman said, gesturing towards the angry waterfall crashing into the valley below.

Margaret lifted her eyebrows, then nodded half-heartedly.

"This your first time in Iceland?"

"Yes," Margaret replied.

"I love this place. First came here on my honeymoon. Before it became all trendy and such. We celebrated our tenth anniversary here too."

Margaret glanced around as if looking for the husband.

"On my own this time, though," the woman said. "Bill died last year."

"I'm sorry."

"This would have been our twentieth. Figured I'd come back one last time, you know, relive some of those memories and say goodbye."

The woman reached into her purse and pulled out a cigarette pack. She held it out to Margaret, who shook her head.

"What about you?" she asked as she took a drag. "You married?" Margaret looked out over the emptiness beyond the waterfall.

Was she?

MARGARET NORMALLY spent her days asking strangers for money for people who'd been knocked down so much they slouched through their lives as if anticipating a rain of blows. She worried at times that all she was doing was dabbing a Kleenex against a spouting jugular vein.

Still, she did what she could.

Until the day her assistant barged into her office just as the major donor Margaret had been courting for months was about to sign the papers. She had an urgent call. Police were swarming their neighbourhood and were inside her house. Margaret grabbed her purse and bolted out the door.

Turning onto her street, she saw police cars everywhere, including one blocking her driveway. She pulled up beside the curb. Her next-door neighbour came rushing over.

"They've taken James," she said. "In handcuffs. What's going on? What's he done?"

Margaret ignored her and charged up the lawn towards the front door. Inside, a half dozen police were traipsing through her house.

"Do you have a lawyer?" her brother, Stuart, asked when she called to tell him what was happening. "You need a lawyer. I know a guy." As if he was a Mafia don arranging a hit.

"They took James."

"Where?"

"I don't know."

"Ask them. They have to tell you."

Instead, she retreated to the den at the back of the house, unable to watch the men in heavy boots pawing through her cupboards and closets. She peered out at the gazebo James had built her the summer before. The blooming peonies surrounding the wooden lattice structure fluttered in the breeze, a smattering of crumpled pink tissue petals falling to the ground.

Then, a policeman carrying a crowbar marched towards the building. Hearing the brutal crunch and squeak of wooden boards being ripped from posts, she grabbed a poker from the fireplace and ran into the yard shaking it at him as if wielding a sword against a marauding army.

"Stop," she screamed. "Leave it alone."

Somebody grabbed her around the shoulders and escorted her back into the house, where she curled up in a ball on the couch in the den. Her phone rang. It was her brother. He told her he'd made an appointment with a lawyer.

"They're tearing my gazebo down," she cried.

"Never mind that. You need to meet with the lawyer today at 2 PM."

"I can't," Margaret said. "I'm going to visit James."

"You most certainly are not."

"I am."

"Do you have any idea...?"

"Yes, I do."

"Hold on. I'm getting Debbie to talk to you."

"Your wife is not going to change my mind."

But, in the end, she wasn't able to face her husband.

Everyone who called that first day assured her it was a big mistake. There was no way James was capable of committing those awful crimes.

Then, he confessed.

He said he did it to spare her.

But it didn't spare her. His claims she knew nothing tainted her with suspicion and fuelled talk of her complicity, as Stuart told her during a tough love talk Margaret did not realize they were having.

After the exodus of those unwilling to risk guilt by association, she was left with a few smug optimists flaunting their pop-up platitudes as if tossing rice at newlyweds to ensure prosperity. Worse than the ones pretending her husband's arrest was nothing more than a minor blip to be surmounted with grit and a can-do attitude, were the ones encouraging her in breathy tones to talk about the sordid details.

Like Hope, an old friend who invited Margaret to stay with her after James's confession.

Just until everything blew over. Margaret didn't know what to do. For the first time ever, she was afraid to be home, alone. Staying with her brother was out of the question and she couldn't bear to face her mother and her disappointment. She would make it all about her. Her fear. Her drama.

Margaret didn't know who else to turn to. So, she accepted Hope's invitation and drove over to her place, not knowing what to expect.

At first, she was stoic, determined not to break down. But Hope, always a fan of the heavy pour, kept the wine coming. The more Margaret drank, the more her resolve to stay strong faltered.

"I can't imagine..." Hope said.

"I know," replied Margaret swallowing another gulp of Merlot.

"What did you think when you heard?"

"I didn't believe it. I thought it was all some twisted misunderstanding. A ploy. A lie. I don't know. Anything that made more sense than the man I've loved for fifteen years, doing those things..." Margaret said, choking on her words.

"It must have been horrible. Did you have any idea, like from how he was with you? Did he ever, you know...?" Hope asked, her eyes widening, hands grasping the stem of her wine glass.

Margaret put her head down on the table. Hope came around and put her hand on her back, but Margaret sloughed it off and stood up. Swaying from the flood of alcohol sloshing through her system, she said, "Will you call me a cab?"

"You don't have to leave..."

"Never mind, I'll do it myself," she said, reaching for her purse.

"No, no, I'll call. Are you sure? Did I upset you?"

"Please. I just want to go home."

When she walked in the front door, her house was in shambles. Caught up in her slurred thoughts about Hope and James, she had forgotten about the police incursion. Evidence of their visit was everywhere. Strewn amongst the fuzzy mice with bells and catnip-laced scratching posts, were trails of dried mud and debris. Drawers were pulled out, furniture dislodged, rugs askew. A couple of the cats ran out mewing. She crouched down and petted them, then picked the closest one up and held him tightly to her chest.

Margaret adopted her first cat, a mottled yellow and black tortoise-shell, after it wandered into the yard one cool spring morning while James was in the Yukon researching his newest mystery series. She named the cat Cumin as a joke, since she lived on Indian takeout whenever James was away.

Next came Poppy, Pepper, Cinnamon, and Ginger. All abandoned cats from the neighbourhood. Then, one day she scurried down a downtown alley, past dumpsters and random pieces of clothing strewn about, chasing a scruffy tom with a torn ear and a cloudy eye. Wading through the greasy aroma of blackened banana peels and the sweet tang of discarded engine oil, she scooped him up, dubbed him Cayenne, and took him home. He couldn't really be loved and have those wounds, she told herself, as she unhooked the leather strap around his neck and tossed it into the trash.

She had tried to avoid the details of James's crimes. Refusing to read the news. Avoiding television, radio, the internet. And yet, still, somehow, she knew too much.

She sifted through her past, looking for clues. But like panning for gold at the base of a waterfall, every time she thought she caught a glimmer of something, it disappeared within the deluge that followed. All those experiences, all those feelings. Which ones were random memories? And which ones were signs?

Standing in the chaos of her overturned living room, she felt an intense urge to flee, to escape her now-tarnished life.

But leaving was a betrayal she wasn't ready to commit.

She pulled out a cloth and liquid cleaner from beneath the kitchen sink. Wiping down the glass coffee table, she was startled by the sight of her distraught reflection, by the smudged image of her disheveled hair, frantic eyes, and drunk shoulders.

Late that night, she was woken by a smashing sound, the tinkle of falling glass, and the roar of a car speeding away. She turned and reached for James. Finding only an empty space, she clutched the covers over her head and lay still, trying to hide from what was happening. When she heard a cat meow, she leapt out of bed, worried it might step on broken glass.

Afraid to turn on the light, she grabbed her phone, using its glow to find a broom so she could clean up the mess before anyone got hurt. After sweeping up the debris, she crumpled on to the rug beside her night table.

When she woke the next morning, curled up in a ball in the corner of her bedroom, she knew she needed to get away. Maybe she could disappear into the hills of Ireland. Spend her days roaming through wild open pastures and along coastal trails that overlooked the harsh North Atlantic Sea. And in the evening, she could linger in country pubs with dark oak panels, quaffing pints of Guinness and wolfing down bangers and mash.

There was a flight to Dublin with a free layover in Iceland leaving in two days. Desperate to do something to shake off the despair threatening to drown her, she bought a plane ticket, then went back to tackling the mess, unable to bear the thought of coming home to the disarray.

They had a woman who came in every week, but Margaret didn't want her seeing the house like this. Besides, she missed the simplicity of doing her own cleaning. Nothing in her job was as straightforward and satisfying as scrubbing a floor until it was spotless. While the effects of cleaning were only ever temporary, at the moment cleanliness was achieved, it could not be improved upon. It was briefly, perfection. And Margaret could use a little perfection.

She scrubbed and sterilized and swept away all signs of the police invasion on the first floor. Standing at the top of the stairs with her cleaning gear, she looked into the dark basement. She'd seen all the boxes they took from James's study and she had not dared to go down.

Steeling herself, she descended the stairs and was overwhelmed by the sight of ceiling tiles removed, furniture pulled from walls, filing cabinet drawers open, their contents scattered about. It was even worse than upstairs. Terrified to think of what they must have found to have torn the place apart like this, she dropped the cloth and pail, grabbed a suitcase from the storage room, and retreated to the living room.

She sank to the floor and sat back against the couch. Chili, her preening Mackerel tabby, ran up and butted her hand with his head. As she petted him, he purred and shimmied and pressed against her. Soon, the others began to circle and meow and clamber over her.

She shooed the cats away, went up to her bedroom, shoved some clothing into her bag, and started gathering her toiletries. Sweeping open the shower curtain, she remembered how James would bury his face in her hair, breathing in the woody citrus smell of her shampoo whenever he came home after being away. She slumped against the wall and wept. Big, loud, earthy sobs. Unlike her usual tears-rolling-down-her-cheek quiet misery.

She grabbed the shampoo container and threw it against the shower wall, its gooey green contents spilling onto the porcelain, a sticky fragrance saturating the air.

FORTY-EIGHT HOURS later, Margaret stood on a rocky Icelandic ledge with a gaggle of tourists watching a torrent of water rush down a battered valley while miles away, below the wind-trashed tundra, the harmonic tremors began.

She returned to the bus, avoiding the inquisitive widow's hopeful gaze by staring at her phone as she squished down the narrow aisle. She'd forgotten about the easy intimacy forged by travellers. Margaret could not afford a new friend right now. So, she walked to her spot near the back, placed her purse on the seat beside her and stared out the window. The diesel engine kicked on, a whoosh of artificial air shooting out the vents above her.

"Sit back, relax, and enjoy the view," said the tour guide as they pulled out of the parking lot. She tried, and for a moment, succeeded. Then she checked her voicemail.

"How many bloody cats do you have?" her brother asked. "Debbie went to your place this morning..."

She deleted Stuart's message and stared out at the stark terrain.

After the waterfall, the next stop on their tour was a crater lake formed from a cone volcano that collapsed into the earth. Surrounded by steep slopes of crumbling red rock with veins of green moss, a quiet cloud-mirroring pool lay at the bottom of a deep bowl.

As the rest of her tour mates advanced towards the site, Margaret continued past the lake onto the barren ground surrounding it. She gazed across the desolate landscape, so pulchritudinous – the perfect ugly word to describe its beauty – the scars from its past lying in plain sight.

A man rushed up to her speaking emphatically in Icelandic and gesticulating towards the sky. She had no idea what he was saying. She froze, staring at the ground, waiting for him to leave. He came closer and she backed away as if he was dangerous. He stopped and spoke again, less violently, but no less urgently.

Then her phone rang.

Margaret had been ignoring her mother's calls but, unsettled by the man shouting at her, she answered without thinking.

"Thank God, I reached you. I've been trying for ages. Where are you?"

"I, uh."

"Oh, Margaret. What are you going to do? I can't imagine. To live with someone all those years...Were there any clues at all?"

"Mom..."

"I know, I know. But there must have been something. Do you have to testify?"

"I don't..."

"Oh, God. What if you lose your job? Do you have any savings? Can they take your house from you?" her mother asked.

Margaret let the cell phone drop away from her ear as she stared out at the harsh, craggy land.

"What's going to happen to you...?"

Margaret flung her phone away. It smashed against a rock.

Ignoring the now-silent man, she marched over to the scattered remains of her phone, scooped up the pieces, shoved them in her bag, and turned back towards the bus. Halfway there, she met the tour guide who was on his way to find her. They were leaving.

As she walked down the aisle to her seat, everyone around her was abuzz with talk of the erupting volcano, of airports being closed. There was a gleeful tinge to the danger chatter, safe as they were from its worst effects. They would be grounded, nothing more. Unable to fly through the ash-choked skies. Unable to move on to wherever they were headed.

Back at the hotel, the tour bus passengers flocked together, giddy with excitement over their shared crisis-not-crisis. Except Margaret, who stepped away from the clusters of chatter and escaped to her room.

She stood at the window and watched the daylight fade. When the sky grew dark, she turned on a lamp and started adjusting random objects around the room, lining up the pen beside the pad of paper, correcting the tilted lampshade, and putting the hotel's welcome binder back onto the desk. Then, she sat on the edge of the bed and stared at the wall. She needed alcohol and she could not bear the thought of drinking alone in a hotel room in Iceland, trapped by a cloud of ash.

MARGARET HAD RECEIVED the email telling her she was terminated, the morning she flew to Iceland. When the news article came out about her yelling at the police for damaging her gazebo, her executive director called. I'm sure you can appreciate that an episode like that by our Director of Development isn't good optics for the organization, he'd said. And you wouldn't want your situation to impact our clients now, would you?

He suggested she resign. She refused.

She called her brother from the airport lounge in Toronto to say she would need to meet with that lawyer after all when she got home. They had no right to fire her.

As she walked down the dreary hotel hallway in Reykjavik, Margaret knew she was never going to make it to Dublin. Sometimes the place you aim for is not the place where you land.

She took the elevator down to the lobby and went into the hotel bar where she sat at a table in the corner and ordered a glass of Cabernet Sauvignon. Endless shots of the erupting volcano played on a TV hanging from the ceiling while Peggy Lee sang, "You give me fever."

The friendly widow entered the bar, strode up to a table of their tour bus compatriots and started regaling them with a story. Margaret noticed the subtle shifting of bodies as the widow waved her arms enthusiastically, the darting glance from one woman to another that quickly switched to a fake smile of interest when the widow turned in her direction.

Margaret had seen that look before. She'd used it herself. It was the perfect weapon for inflicting damage without getting blood on your hands.

There are so many ways to destroy a person.

The widow saw Margaret, waved at her, and came over to her table.

"I thought it was you. Isn't this the craziest thing? Getting stuck here? All very glamorous. It's a far cry from the record wheat harvest headlines that pass for excitement back home. Where are you from anyway?"

"Toronto."

"Get out of town," the woman said, slapping the top of the table. "I should have known you were Canadian. Me too! Not exactly a downtown girl though. Yorkton, Saskatchewan. I won't even ask if you've been there. Nobody ends up in Yorkton unless they're born there, or they run out of gas on their way to someplace else. Had any car trouble in the Prairies lately? Ha. Ha. There are a few other Canadians around. A couple from your neck of the woods. Oshawa maybe? I'm Gladys, by the way. Mind if I join you?"

"No, yes, I uh, I have to leave. I'm meeting a friend."

"You know someone who lives here?"

Margaret stood up abruptly.

"Sorry. I've just...I've got to go now."

She hurried into the lobby and approached the front desk clerk to get an update on her flight. He pointed to a flip chart they'd set up with the latest cancellation information. For now, no planes were coming in or going out. Margaret stared intently at the TV in the lobby as if waiting for a different outcome to magically appear. Eventually, she gave up, and went back to her room. She slipped into the elevator ahead of a small crowd coming out of the bar. A pair of women from her tour bus boarded at the last second and turned to the front without glimpsing Margaret who was hidden behind a stout man.

"I heard her husband killed himself. In the barn with a rifle. And she was the one to find him."

"Sad."

"Though you'd never know it the way she carries on with that cheerful widow schtick. I can't help wondering what she..." The women's voices faded as they stepped out into the hallway.

The doors closed and with a slight shudder, the elevator continued its climb upwards.

Suddenly, Margaret could not bear to face the contrived neatness of her hotel room, the excessive orderliness of the minimalist Scandinavian furniture and tiny angular paintings of geometric figures, which only accentuated the room's underlying bleakness. She returned to the lobby and headed outside where she found Gladys smoking alone at the front of the hotel.

"You off to see your friend?"

Margaret felt a dizzying swirl of guilt and compassion for this woman who smiled at her as if she was a decent person.

"Could I bum a smoke?" Margaret asked.

"Sure. Of course. I didn't know you were a smoker."

"I'm not. There are times even we non-smokers need a cigarette."

"That's for sure true," Gladys said as she held out her lighter to Margaret. "I used to only smoke socially. You know, one of those annoying people who bum cigarettes from their friends when they're out drinking. After my husband died, I started smoking like a damn chimney. I needed to do something to keep myself busy. Just when the shock of his death was turning into full-on grief, the ones who'd been there at the beginning with their cards and their casseroles all went back to their regular lives. Then when people started hearing talk that Bill killed himself, well.... there's some that feel that kind of tragedy's contagious. Like a virus that'll infect you if you come too close."

Margaret shook her head.

"I mean, I get it," Gladys continued. "It's scary stuff. That's why

I didn't get mad when people stopped coming by or slipped down a different aisle when they saw me in the grocery store. And I sure the hell didn't care when they forgot to invite me to a damn bake sale or some such thing I didn't give two hoots about anyway."

"That's awful," Margaret blurted out.

"It's just sad, you know," Gladys said, shrugging. "You think people have your back. And when they're not there for you like you thought they would be, like they thought they would be, well, nobody comes out of that feeling good about themselves."

"No, I guess not," Margaret said, taking a deep drag on her cigarette. "Do you have kids?"

"Nope. You?"

"Uh uh. I have cats. You got any pets?"

"Never saw much point in them," Gladys replied. "I grew up on a farm. Animals weren't allowed inside the house. We had barn cats to keep the rats down. When you got a lot of animal feed around, you get a lot of rats."

"My cats give me such comfort," said Margaret.

"I could never get used to all the dead birds. I was always stumbling across clumps of feathers everywhere."

Margaret did spend a lot of time cleaning up after her cats. Sweeping away the puffs of hair that littered the floor and the bed and the counters. Wiping up clumps of vomit or gathering the mangled rodent and robin bits they dropped in front of her, like rose petals strewn by a suitor.

"I had this one cat," Margaret said, "who brought me the headless body of a mouse every day for a week. We didn't even have mice in our house. It was clearly hunting for them elsewhere and bringing them home."

Gladys nodded and smiled sadly at her.

Margaret saw it then. The pity in her eyes. She knew.

"I have to go," Margaret mumbled, throwing her burning cigarette to the ground and stumbling off into the night.

A few blocks away, she went inside an Internet café and Googled his name. There it was. A picture of him. With her. On the front page of

The Toronto Sun. It was taken at a neighbour's barbecue, smoke from the grill swirling into the top corner of the photo. James held a paper plate with a hamburger and potato salad while she clutched white wine in a plastic glass, her head thrown back in laughter at something outside the frame.

She shut down the browser, stumbled out of the café and crouched against the wall, unable to breathe. Gasping, she slapped at her chest until she could inhale once more.

The images she had tried to avoid, but could never escape, infected her thoughts. The women. His victims. The shame, like acid devouring her insides. And now this picture out in the world, linking them together. Irrevocably. Forever.

Love is an act of faith we hope will never be tested.

But now that it had been, what was she supposed to do? How was she was supposed to feel? All those years, she thought she knew him. She loved him. Still. Maybe. She wasn't sure. Could she love a part of him?

Wasn't that all we ever did?

And what about the rest of her fucked-up feelings? The horror, the repugnance, the shame. What was she supposed to do with the air-sucking, skin-scalding, roaring flame of fury ripping through her veins?

She stood up slowly and headed deeper into the city, away from the hotel. Reykjavik was quiet. Unlike Toronto's constant bustle and clatter. There was nothing to distract her from her anguish as she rambled the city streets.

She didn't know where she was or how long she'd been walking when she saw a concrete building with the universal Ladies silhouette painted on the front. Inside, she locked the door and went straight to the mirror, her skin a ghostly hue under the fluorescent lights. She pulled a lipstick from her bag and ran it along dry cracked lips.

A tidy woman falling apart does not leave behind a dignified ruin. She's more like the chaotic collapse of a building in wartime, puffs of dried dust rising from the rubble.

Margaret yanked a handful of toilet paper from the dispenser and swiped the colour from her mouth. Her heart bruised, her stomach tight, she stared at her slouching reflection.

She was not guilty.

Which was not the same as being innocent.

She closed her eyes and breathed deeply, trying to relax, to regain her calm. She just wanted to go back to the hotel and crawl into bed.

Turning away from the mirror, she reached for the lock on the bathroom door. It was stuck.

She yanked and pushed and kicked. But it wouldn't budge. Banging her fists against the metal door in time with the frantic thumping of her heart, she yelled for help. Nothing. She slid to the floor.

She was trapped in a toilet in Iceland, her cellphone in pieces at the bottom of her bag, her husband locked up in jail far away.

She lifted her head.

Nobody knew where she was. Which meant no one could reach her.

A dirty relief washed over her.

She began to laugh. And she kept laughing.

Unable to stop.

Hummingbirds

DUST CATCHES on Lauren's runners as she dashes down the dry dirt road.

The steady thump of her feet on the earth disrupts the pinging images she's trying to outrun. A falling body. Flashing lights. Lovely lanky boys in scrubs. A caustically clean hallway.

Her mind clears as her strength falters.

Slowing to a walk, she bends over and clutches her knees. She breathes deeply to slow her racing pulse, then turns down the laneway of her grandparents' lake house where her mother and sisters are gathered around a bonfire.

Lauren collapses on the ground and stares up at the sky, at the hint of stars lurking on the edge of the disappearing daylight. The warmth of the beach soothes her aching muscles as she sweeps the palms of her hands away from her sides, creating angel wings in the sand.

"How was your run?" her mother, Olivia, asks. "Grace, stop that."

"I want to see if it catches fire."

"Well, it won't. And if you keep it up, the fire will go out and you won't be able to roast marshmallows."

Grace tosses the sand still clutched in her fist at her younger sister Ella.

"Mom," Ella cries.

"That's enough, Grace. Lauren, go check on Grandma."

"In a minute."

"Now. See if you can get her to come down."

Lauren struggles to her feet, stomping on the ground to settle her cramping legs. She heads towards the house while her mother helps Ella and Grace load their marshmallow sticks.

"And tell her to bring Grandpa's ashes."

OLIVIA GRIEVES for her father, though not as much as she thinks she should. He tried to stop her from marrying Dave. She never forgave him for that. Nor did she forgive herself for defying him. He'd been right. But then...the girls.

Ella and Grace pluck at the charred marshmallows, stripping the paper-thin black crust and wrapping their mouths around the melty blob beneath. With sticky fingers and gooey sugar-coated teeth, they tumble into Olivia's lap, jabbing her breasts and thighs with their jostling elbows.

As if lured by the smell of burnt sugar, a hummingbird flits around them. Ella and Grace jump up and shout, "Grandpa, Grandpa."

The hummingbird flies backwards from their exuberance then soars off in search of something more than the whisper of sustenance.

"Is Grandpa coming back?" Ella asks.

"No, honey, he can't. He's gone now."

"But if he's a hummingbird, he could fly back here, easy."

"Maybe," says Olivia, pulling their fidgeting bodies close.

Grace, who hates showers, smells like warm pennies buried in a child's fist while Ella is all honeysuckle and oranges. Olivia squeezes her daughters. They burrow into her warmth as a crisp breeze blows across their still damp skin.

Her daughters' steady pulses tamp Olivia's burbling panic, the panic normally buried beneath the rat-a-tat call of tantrums and starburst cries of the young. She is grateful for the demands of messy childish emotions. For their distraction from her ailing car, her lost husband, her dead dad.

LAUREN STEPS INTO the cool interior of the house, the living room dreary and dark against the twilight tinged outdoors. Her grandmother, Lucille, sits in an easy chair facing the window, her hands lying across the cardboard box on her lap.

Lauren has spent every summer with her grandparents since she was five. The early years were blissful. Then her father moved back home and soon after, two new sisters appeared. The youngest, Ella, looks like Lauren, the same copper hair and smattering of freckles like a constellation of stars across her face. Grace is the product of a different batch of cookie dough, a dark-haired howling dervish.

Her sisters are so much younger than her, it's as if they're on loan from another family. Except they stayed.

"Why can't Ella and Grace go live with Dad?" she asked her mom soon after her father ran off with his best friend's daughter to Thailand, where they started a travel agency specializing in diving vacations.

At least she'd still had her grandfather to herself. Even after her sisters started tagging along, he focused most of his attention on Lauren. She was older. She could do things they couldn't.

Every day he woke her up at 6 AM for an early morning swim. Even when it was cold. Even when there were whitecaps on the waves. Even when she buried her head under the covers and refused to go out.

He wanted her to be a lawyer like him. She wanted to be a hip-hop dancer or a synchronized swimmer. Only her grandmother considered those viable career options.

He spent hours teaching her Ping-Pong, including how to unleash a wicked topspin. She thought he would be impressed when she started to win.

Instead, he stopped playing with her.

LUCILLE STROKES the package containing the remains of her husband as Lauren wanders into the room.

"The thing about your grandfather..." Lucille says, holding her index finger in the air before disappearing into a moment, her gaze high and vague, her hand drooping.

Howard grew up with his mother in a decrepit luxury apartment in the Annex after his father, a millionaire carpet magnate, lost all their money in a Swedish Ponzi scheme and then disappeared on a trek to the Arctic. Howard started working as a shoeshine boy in Toronto's subway tunnels at thirteen. Lucille had never known a more driven man.

"Did you know your grandfather and I met when I starred in a play at Stratford?" Lucille says, picking up her dangling thread at a different spot.

"Yes, Grandma, you told me."

"I was quite the looker in those days. When I walked into a room, everyone stopped and stared. Only your grandpa had the guts to talk to me. More than that, he wooed me. There's not many women who can resist being wooed, even if they have other plans."

Lucille dreamed of a life in the theatre. Growing up as a dusty farm girl with six older brothers, she spent her childhood performing self-penned plays for a barn full of lowing Holsteins, and her adolescence sidestepping a bevy of boys wanting to slip a marriage bridle on her.

After getting pregnant with Olivia, there were no more star turns at Stratford or anywhere else. The closest Lucille got to another leading role was the summer she roped Lauren into putting on a show for the family. Her granddaughter danced a krump routine she copied from a YouTube video while Lucille resurrected a soliloquy from *A Doll's House* that she'd performed years before. Their closing act was a rousing rendition of Cabaret culminating in a chorus line of two doing a slow motion can-can to a standing ovation.

At least she'd managed to inject a touch of flair into her role as dutiful wife and mom. And she'd taken to the part of naughty Grandma with a cheeky glee that surprised even her. One Friday afternoon she snuck Lauren into a matinee of *All that Jazz* after forging a note from Olivia allowing Lauren out of a math test for a "critically vital dental appointment."

"How can you become a dancer without experiencing Bob Fosse?" she reasoned.

When Olivia found out, she grounded Lauren and threatened to cancel her visit to her grandparents that summer. Lucille knew Olivia didn't have a choice. She had to work and couldn't afford to hire anyone to watch the kids, especially after Dave started bailing on his alimony payments. Apparently, it was harder to make money running diving tours in Phuket than he'd anticipated.

Lucille reaches for Lauren's hand and leads her out to the wrap-around balcony on the opposite side of the house from Olivia and the girls. Setting the cardboard box on the railing, she scoops out two handfuls of ash and holds her clenched fists to her chest. She nods at Lauren who hesitates before reaching into the box.

They both stand at the railing, closed hands held in front of them.

"One, two, three...Goodbye my sweet warrior," Lucille says, as they thrust their arms forward, fists springing open.

Particles and powder fly into the air, some of the lighter flecks drifting back and landing on Lauren's arm.

"It's so hard," she says, her eyes welling from the grit, from the finality.

"It's your first time losing someone, sweetie. It's supposed to be hard."

"I can't believe he's never coming back," Lauren says, tears falling as she rubs tiny flakes of her grandfather into her skin.

"I know, honey. When you love somebody, it's like a sliver is buried deep in your heart and you never know when it's going to rise to the surface and make you bleed." She pats her granddaughter's arm. "But it's worth it."

"Now, take this to your mother," she says, handing Lauren the box. "Let her do what she needs to do. Go on."

Lucille returns to the living room and settles into a chair by the window, her arthritic bones grateful for the succor of a soft cushion. Alone in the dark, her mind drifts down the back lanes of a prettified past. Meandering through a landscape of memories blurred by the wearying weight of time and the clouding of aging eyes, she is free to create her own story.

Even if just for her.

Even if muddled and not quite true.

OLIVIA COUNTED on her father once. That illusion was ripped away the day she saw a car getting T-boned by a Chevy running a stop sign.

The man who got hit was lucky. His car was totaled but he was not badly hurt. The driver of the Chevy flew through his windshield and was a crumpled bloody mess on the road when Howard crouched down beside him.

Olivia and her father had been on their way to a Jewel concert. She was too young to go alone, and he volunteered to take her. Instead of swaying to the melodic lilt of poetic yearnings and earnest guitars, Olivia watched, horrified, as her father pressed hard on the driver's chest to staunch the bleeding. Then, he lifted the man's upper body and just held him, his head drooping against Howard's chest.

Her father was not able to save the man. And he was not able to shield Olivia from watching the man die in his arms.

"I'm fine," she'd said, when he touched her shoulder, the blood on his hands not quite erased by a rough scrub with the dog's blanket he found stowed in the trunk of his car.

LAUREN SLIDES THE GLASS door open and steps outside, the beach awash in the quiet glow of the fading sun. She feels as though her skin is turned inside out; her entire body one large exposed nerve.

She'd been surprised at how coarse and lumpy her grandfather's ashes were, and that she could feel him in the dust she held in the palm of her hand, a subtle pulse of life where there should be none.

She was alone with him when he fell. She'd tried to wake him. Then she and her grandmother were riding through the night in an ambulance with the siren wailing. Two young men in blue scrubs wheeled him down a hallway that smelt of ammonia and decay.

Lauren walks towards her sisters who huddle near the fire wrapped tight in faded old towels.

"Grandpa's back," cries Ella as the hummingbird returns, its shimmering colours a flare against the deepening dusk.

"Where's Grandma?" asks Olivia.

"She's not coming. But she gave me his ashes."

Lauren hands the container to her mother who glances at her father's remains with faraway eyes.

"Grandma's a drama queen," says Grace, parroting one of her mother's snide asides.

"Shut up, Grace," says Lauren.

"Hey, hey, none of that," Olivia says.

"She's so rude."

"What? I didn't do anything."

"Grandpa just died and you're saying stupid things," says Lauren.

"Alright, that's enough, both of you. What shall we do with Grandpa's ashes?"

"Throw them in the air and make a wish."

"They're not birthday candles, Ella," Olivia says. "Lauren?"

"I don't care."

"How about sprinkling them in the lake? Wouldn't that be nice for Grandpa?"

"Yes, yes," holler Ella and Grace.

"I want to do it."

"No, it's my turn," says Grace as if Ella always gets to scatter the family's ashes. The girls tussle. Grief is given short shrift by the young.

"You can each do some. What about you, Lauren?"

"Don't you even care that he's dead?" Lauren asks.

"Of course, I do."

"You don't act like it."

"What are you talking about?"

"It's like he's just a speck of dust floating away. No big deal."

"Don't be so dramatic," Olivia says, pulling Ella onto her lap.

"Look, he's back," says Grace, pointing to the flitting blur above their heads.

"Grandpa, Grandpa," calls Ella, then falls back against her mother's chest and closes her eyes.

"DO YOU NEED MONEY?" Howard asked one weekend, after Olivia's divorce was finalized.

"Always," she replied. "But no, Dad, I'm managing."

"You should be doing more than just managing by now."

"I'm doing the best I can."

"I know. And I worry."

"Well, don't."

"It's not that easy."

"Nothing ever is. And yet here we are."

She should have been able to move on after witnessing the car accident. And she did. Sort of. All through high school she dated recklessly. Bad boys, good boys, boys who didn't know who they were going to be. Lurking beneath the surface, there was always that precarity, that uncertainty, that speeding Chevy ready to slam into her life. Her father had always been her superhero. Watching him behave so courageously in real life, only to fail, unsettled her. If he couldn't protect her, why should she listen to him? So, she stopped. Even when she knew she was being foolish. Even when it hurt. It became a habit she could not muster the energy to break.

And now that he's gone, she misses that long-ago belief that he could save her.

LAUREN TURNS AWAY from her mother and sisters, away from the glare of the hummingbird's beauty and continuance. The skin where she ground her grandfather's ashes burns like a rash and the rough particles wedged beneath her nails create a prickly throbbing in her fingers.

Distracted by Ella and Grace, her mother does not notice her walking into the water. Lauren skims the surface of the lake in a shallow dive and swims hard towards the horizon. Kicking past cold, she seeks the solace of pure exhaustion.

Lost in the rhythm of her strokes, she doesn't hear her mother call until glancing at the flat line ahead she realizes she's gone too far. Pausing, she sweeps her hands beneath the surface, the water lifting and lowering her in its gentle flow.

Letting her mother's voice pull her back, she returns to the bristling beach, her sisters running and somersaulting across the moonlit sand. A glistening trail of tears and water streams down her chilled flesh as she plops onto the ground, crosses her arms in front of her chest and shivers by the fire.

Olivia sits down beside her daughter and drapes a towel around her, pulling her stiff body close. Lauren fights the urge to drop her head onto her mother's shoulder. She is not yet ready to be comforted.

Like a hummingbird entering torpor to prevent starvation caused by its incessantly beating wings, she closes her eyes to stem the flow of time, to stave off the cascade of misery threatening to consume her.

Still, the dead remain dead, the future devours the past, and the children dance and twirl against the fading day.

Acknowledgements

Thank you to the St. John's writing community and its supporters. To be able to spend time with, and benefit from, so many talented local writers has been an incredible opportunity. And to live in a city where attending literary and other cultural events is a natural part of life is inspiring.

I am grateful for every writer, friend, and acquaintance who read my work along the way. But I would like to specifically thank those who provided crucial feedback, support, and kindness, including my writing group who graciously allowed this anti-social, awkward human being to join them.

Thank you to Heidi Wicks, Kelley Power, Jennifer McVeigh, Matthew Hollett, Penny Hansen, Carmella Gray-Cosgrove, Terry Doyle, Amy Donovan, Bridget Canning, Sharon Bala, and Angela Antle.

Thank you also to Susie Taylor for her input, advice, and friendship.

And a huge thank you to Lisa Moore for her extraordinary contributions to the writing community in Newfoundland and Labrador generally, and for her generous encouragement and support of my work specifically. We are so fortunate to have her as a leading force of the writing community and I am beyond grateful for all she has done and continues to do.

I would also like to acknowledge the Writers Association of Newfoundland and Labrador (WANL) and the creative writing department of Memorial University of Newfoundland and Labrador for their ongoing support of writers in this province. I benefited greatly from the classes, workshops, and programs offered by both organizations and I am most appreciative of all the writers who provided their knowledge and expertise within these programs.

Thank you to Debra Bell and John Kennedy at Radiant Press for taking a chance on me. I am thrilled that you published my book and it's been an absolute pleasure working with you. Thank you to Susan Musgrave for her insightful editorial input and to everyone else at Radiant who has contributed to the creation, distribution, and promotion of this book.

To my mother, Patricia Carley, who always encouraged my writing and whose ongoing artistic endeavours while being a single mom raising three daughters served as a quiet inspiration for the creative life.

And thank you to the friends and family I have not mentioned by name. You are all deeply a part of me and have contributed immensely to my life and as such, have contributed to this book.

Finally, thank you to my partner Sarah Martin for her never-ending support and for being a part of this adventure of a life we've shared all these years. You are a wonder, and I am so grateful to be on this journey with you.

Diane Carley has worked in a variety of jobs across Canada including office manager in a fish plant, behavioural classroom aide, vocational counsellor, mental health worker, project manager, and librarian. Her writing has appeared in *The Antigonish Review*, *subTerrain*, *The Fiddlehead*, *Riddle Fence*, and *The Globe and Mail*, among other publications. She lives in St. John's, NL.